N   LvER

DAMAGED HERO

KELLY MOORE

Edited by
KERRY GENOVA

Illustrated by
DARK WATER COVERS

NEVER EVER

NEVER EVER

BESTSELLING AUTHOR
KELLY MOORE

Copyright © 2023 by Kelly Moore

All rights reserved.

No part of this book may be reproduced in any form or by any electronic or mechanical means, including information storage and retrieval systems, without written permission from the author, except for the use of brief quotations in a book review.

❀ Created with Vellum

1 NOA

The day is as stormy as I feel on the inside. People hustle and bustle around me throughout the subway station as if I were nonexistent, which has been my state of mind for the past two years of my life. Do they sense it? Or are they so wrapped up in their own world that no one else matters?

As the train halts on the platform, I squeeze inside like cattle being herded through a small gate. The bench seats fill up quickly, and I opt to grab onto the leather hand loops dangling from the ceiling. Once the doors close, the stagnate air fills with a mix of perfume and cologne, along with some scent I'd rather not think about. As I read the posters and bright advertisements pinned along the top of the walls, I notice no one makes eye contact. Heads are buried in phones, eyes closed, listening to the music in their earbuds, watching videos, reading books, or pretty much whatever it takes to kill time until they reach their destination.

A voice comes over the speaker, announcing the next stop, and the train bolts forward. I tighten my grip so as not to get in someone else's space. A hard task considering we're within inches of one another. A lady in the back wearing a pirate hat garners my attention when she starts speaking in a loud voice about the end of days, telling anyone who will listen that she has a spaceship in her backyard that will save us all.

Thus one of the many reasons why I dislike New York City so much. I've never been a fan of big cities, and right about now, I want to flee back to Essex and never leave the comfort of my home. In fact, stay buried in my bed. Peace and quiet have been my sanctuary when I've needed it the most.

I flinch when a cold, small hand touches mine. I look down to see a tiny girl with round eyes the color of an ocean in the Caribbean. Either that, or I'm imagining the shade of blue because it brings me warmth in the dampness of this day. She traces her fingertips over my silver ring that's become too loose this past year. She stops spinning it to take a closer look at the heart-shaped ring with a diamond in the middle of it. It was a gift from my late husband. The thought of him lodges a lump in my throat.

"It's so pretty." Her lashes bat against her soft cheeks when she peers at me with a wide smile baring missing teeth.

"Thank you. It's very special to me," I respond, returning her grin.

"Leave the lady alone," the woman standing next to her, who I assume is her mother, says.

"It's alright. She wasn't bothering me," I assure her.

A child is something that Drake and I never got around to, and now that he's gone, the possibility of me having a son or daughter died with him. He was too focused on his career and kept putting me off. I agreed because my career as a food critic blogger had me traveling more than I was home, and if I'm truly honest with myself, I felt the timing wasn't right either.

The girl's hand drifts away from mine and into her mother's when I notice how tattered her clothes are, and her shoes appear worn and too large for her feet. The zipper on the woman's purse is hanging on by a thread, and stains cover the sleeves of her shirt. I feel privileged in comparison and want to help them. It's just another thing I dislike about the city. It's a place with extreme wealth as much as poverty, and it breaks my heart to see a child in need.

Without being too obvious, I fumble to open my wallet in my purse and pull out what cash I have on hand. When the doors open, her attention is drawn away from me, and I slip the money into the opening of her bag and quickly follow a couple out of the train to a busy street in Manhattan.

Tugging my jacket closed and covering my head with the hood of my raincoat, I play a child's game of leapfrog, dodging the puddles of water on the sidewalk. I wait for the crosswalk to give the all clear to move with the crowd of people. The freshly baked bread in a bakery smells heavenly, and a line of people are squeezing their way inside. It's new since the last time I visited this neighborhood. As I make my way down the block, several stores are boarded up with signs posting what's coming next and barricaded by plastic sheets marking a construction zone. There's a restaurant in every nook and cranny, crammed into small spaces. Food vendors are tucked in narrow alleyways. A man mashing his head against his shoulder to hold his phone profusely apologizes to me when he bumps into me without breaking his pace.

I never understood why Drake wanted to open a restaurant in downtown Manhattan with all the competition, but it had always been his dream, so this is where it all started. He got a sweet deal on a prime piece of real estate and spent every dime he'd saved and then some into purchasing it. He borrowed enough money to remodel the century-old tall brick building, bringing it back to life but keeping it as authentic as possible.

I pause at the entrance of The Italian Oven. I used to feel so much pride every time I walked into the place and saw my husband in all his glory mingling with the customers, laughing, and enjoying a toast. Today, all I feel is a deep, saddening loss, and I wish I didn't have to be here.

One step inside, and the marvelous scent of Italian herbs has my mouth watering. It looks exactly like it did two years ago. The same maître d' and bartender who Drake employed as soon as the restaurant opened five years ago are working, and they've since married.

Bruno's smile lights up from behind the bar as soon as he recognizes me. "Noa!" he bellows in his

Italian accent, drowning out voices in the high-ceiling, open room.

Gia confines me in a hug before her husband can snare me in his wide-open hairy arms. "Sofia told me you were coming for a visit. It's so good to see you."

"My sister never could keep a secret." I laugh. "And it's not exactly a visit."

"How long are you in town for?" Bruno kisses both of my cheeks.

"Hopefully not long." My smile fades, recalling why I left New York. "Sofia said she needed me here in person to go over some issue and insisted she couldn't discuss it over the phone, so however long that takes."

"We'd love to have you over for a glass of wine or two." Gia tucks her arm around Bruno's waist. "I want to hear all about your life in Massachusetts."

"Trust me, it's completely boring."

"That's exactly why you need to move back to Manhattan." Sofia's soprano voice rings out loud enough for everyone to hear as she runs toward me, engulfing me in her arms. "You should have told me when you were coming. I could've sent someone to pick you up at the airport."

"I had to do it last minute, or I would've talked

myself out of it. You made it seem very important that I be here, so here I am."

"Just wanting my sister to come for a visit wasn't enough?" she snorts, releasing me. "Let me take your jacket." She tugs my arms out, and I couldn't stop her even if I wanted to.

"I'll pour you a glass of your favorite wine." Bruno steps away, walking back over to the bar.

"We'll catch up later," Gia sings and sways her hips to greet a couple waiting at the door.

"Business appears to be great," I say, looking around at all the customers sitting at tables and on barstools.

"It's picked up a bit since the downturn in the economy. We used to have a waiting list out for a month. Now it's only a week."

"You've done a great job keeping the restaurant afloat. I can't tell you how much I appreciate all your hard work."

She laces her arm with mine, and we walk in front of the large brick pizza oven. "You can thank me by moving back and helping me run this place."

"You know I can't do that. I've been thinking more and more about selling it."

"Oh, sweetie, just give yourself more time. I don't want you to have regrets about selling it. There are so many good memories here, and Drake lived and breathed every inch of this restaurant."

Sometimes I think he loved it more than he did me. He'd spend every waking hour of every day in this place. The last year he was alive, we barely spent any time together with our opposite schedules. I had to beg him to take a vacation with me to St. Lucia. The first two days, he couldn't get off the phone. He was so angry at me when I tossed his cell phone into the blue waters.

It was worth it, though, because the next three days I spent in his arms. It was like when we first met in college. We were inseparable and couldn't get enough of each other until we graduated from Boston College. He'd always known what he wanted and was able to obtain it faster than either one of us had planned. I was working for a magazine, reviewing restaurants, and making decent money. He was employed at a bank, hating every minute of it.

We thought it would take ten years to save enough to make his dreams come true, but tragically, his parents were killed in a car accident. Being an only child, he inherited their insurance policy, and combined with what he had saved, it left him enough to pay for a good portion of this property.

"It houses lots of bad ones too," I say softly, finally working my way through my thoughts.

Bruno hands both of us a glass of wine. "I opened a new bottle, and it's all yours."

"Thanks." I sip and relish the flavor. I haven't had a glass of it since Drake's funeral.

"I've got a few things I need to take care of, and then I'll join you for some appetizers." Sofia tips her glass to mine. "We'll talk business later," she adds as if she read my mind, knowing I'd want all the details this instant.

As much as I love my sister and have missed her, I'd like to get back home as soon as possible.

"I took the liberty of ordering your favorite food items." Bruno points to a high-top table nestled in the bar area.

"You're too good to me." I smile. "And I'm starving, so thank you."

"Enjoy." He walks to the table and pulls out the chair for me before he skates off to tend the bar.

I look around, taking in the customers. An older couple sits in the corner holding hands and appears to be celebrating some occasion. A large table of women laughing and enjoying their food crowd the center of the room. A table of men wearing suits catches my attention. The older gentleman at the table has salt-and-pepper hair and deep wrinkles around his brown eyes. One of the men looks irritated; his jaw is rocking back and forth, looking like he's talking under his breath as the toe of his polished shoe taps the tile floor.

My gaze shifts to the other man who's staring back at me with mesmerizingly intense emerald-green eyes, the color of which I've never seen before. His jet-black hair is neatly groomed over the collar of his pressed shirt, and he has a jawline that would have any woman longing to be in his arms. *Any woman but me, that is.* I've succumbed to my widow status at the ripe old age of thirty-two. I have no intention of entertaining the idea of being in another man's arms, but lord I miss having sex.

His chair screeches across the tile when he stands and excuses himself, and I'm taken off guard when he slowly, with loads of confidence, strides in my direction. I find the way his body moves very sexy, and it stirs my libido.

Moving my head from side to side, I look to see if there is anyone else around me he might be marching toward. When he reaches my table, he stops and gazes at me with a sexy grin. "I haven't seen you in here before."

"It's been a while since I've walked through

these doors." I straighten my spine to feebly match his broad shoulders nearly bursting from his expensive GQ-style suit that probably cost more than my car. A strand of hair falls haphazardly on his forehead, and for some reason, it makes me smile. I stick out my hand. "Noa Sutton," I introduce myself.

He squints. "Sutton," he repeats my last name. "Any relationship to the man that used to own this joint?"

My smile fades, and my heart thuds with ache. "He's my late husband." I don't know that I'll ever get used to that term.

"I'm so sorry." Instead of shaking my hand, he shoves it deep into his pocket. "I love The Italian Oven. It's my favorite place to eat in Manhattan. I come here at least once a month, if not more."

"I didn't catch your name."

"Ever Christianson."

"That's very unusual." I grin.

"I get that a lot." His smile is panty-melting gorgeous. "Have dinner with me."

"Seems to me you already have a dinner date or two."

"None as beautiful as you."

"This seat is taken," Bruno abruptly interrupts us,

crossing his arms over his chest in a protective stance.

Ever's gaze darts between the two of us, and his teeth dig into his bottom lip. "It was very nice to meet you, Noa," he says, walking backward.

"What's got you so hot and bothered?" I touch Bruno's arm.

"He comes in here once a month with those two men who are no good. I don't know what they do, but Drake always broke out in a sweat when they would dine here. He's only been coming with them this past year, but if he's keeping company with those two, I'd advise you to steer clear."

"Thanks for the heads-up, but you don't have to worry about me. I'm not interested. As soon as my sister gets to the point of why I'm here, I'll be gone." I glance around him back to the table of men and see the corner of Ever's mouth lift, then shift his gaze to the older gentleman whose face is scrunched in a scowl, and he's talking with his hands.

"I know you loved your husband, but you need a life of your own. Holing up in Essex away from the people that love you can't be good for your soul."

I reach out and squeeze his hand. "I'm doing just fine." *Fine*. I repeat the word in my head. Most days, I'm barely getting by. I haven't traveled since Drake was murdered other than to leave New York and go back home where I felt safe.

Sipping my wine between bites of stuffed mushrooms, I sweep my gaze around the restaurant, but it keeps landing back on Ever Christianson. He's wickedly handsome when he smiles at me but equally as menacing when his jaw locks in place, listening to the older man.

Sofia pulls out the adjacent chair and joins me. "This is the first time I've gotten to sit down all day." She sighs and pops a mushroom in her mouth.

"These are as good as I recall." I lick my fingertips. "Drake's grandmother sure knew how to cook, and I'm glad she shared her recipes."

"I remember the blog you wrote about these babies. I was drooling over them just reading about them in the article, but I do recollect you got accused of nepotism over it."

"Yeah, until I shoved a mushroom into the asshole's mouth. It shut him right up, and he ordered the appetizer every time he showed his face in here. Her lasagna is to die for too," I hum.

"You didn't come here to be a food critic," she snorts.

"Why am I here?" I tap the rim of my wineglass with my latte-colored fingernails.

"We can wait and discuss it later." She tries to wave me off.

"Now is as good of a time as any. If we get done soon enough, I could catch the redeye out of town."

"I've missed you so much. Why can't you just hang around for a few days? I'll even schedule some time off if you'll stick around. We could take in a show or two."

"You know how much this place hurts." My lip quivers, and I blink back tears before they can spill out.

"Noa," she says my name softly. "You didn't die when Drake did, but you act like it. You've always been so full of life. I hate seeing you like this. New York didn't kill your husband. Bad men did."

"Men that have never paid the price," I mutter.

"Drake would want you to move on, and so do I."

"Can you please just tell me why I'm here?"

She huffs and stands. "Alright, follow me."

We weave our way to the back of the restaurant to what used to be Drake's old office. He was hardly ever in it because he always wanted his face seen by the clients.

Sofia unlocks a filing cabinet and rubs her forehead. "I don't know how much you know about the financing of this place, but there's a large amount of monies due in two weeks."

"What do you mean? We pay a monthly amount to the bank."

She flips open the file. "There was a secondary note taken out the second year we were open to help pay for the remodeling loan and overhead. The place was still struggling, and Drake was fighting to keep it afloat."

"How did I not know this?" I spin the file in my direction.

"It was a loan by an investor, and he's calling for it to be paid. I received this letter a week ago." She points to the page I'm reading.

"Do we have that kind of money?"

"Well, if you were actively involved in the restaurant like you should be, you'd know that we're profitable, but we don't have that much money in reserve. Every expense is already allocated for the year, minus any mishaps."

I exhale, finding my ass in the chair. "I'm sorry. I left everything in your capable hands and knew you'd manage it well. Drake always said you were the one who made things work around here."

"This"—she presses her finger to the numbers on

the page—"I can't make this kind of payment without putting us out of business."

I close my eyes tightly, and when I open them, the only thing I can see is the picture behind Sofia on the wall. It's of Drake and me on a sailboat in St. Lucia. My heart lurches at how much I miss his handsome face.

"Are you listening to me?" She twists around to see what I'm fixated on. "I'm sorry. I should've taken it down." Sofia reaches for it, but I'm on my feet, stopping her.

"No. Pictures of him are all I have left." I stand on my tiptoes, taking it down and clutching it to my chest.

2 EVER

I enjoy the food at The Italian Oven, but I greatly dislike the men I'm eating with...my father and my half brother, who is and always will be a sharp pain in my ass.

"I had my source put a stop to the investigation on our business," my father snaps between bites of lasagna.

"That either means you blackmailed them, or their bodies are floating in a river somewhere." I wipe my hands on the white linen napkin in my lap.

"Would you rather he just slap their hands?" my brother Nick clamors.

"As a matter of fact, I would. Why is killing someone always your go-to method of solving a problem?" I lock my jaw in place.

"Because that's how Leones handle things, and people respect that," my brother snarls.

"By respect, you mean you instill fear in them. You're sadly mistaken if you think you're esteemed by anyone." I let out a short, harsh laugh.

"You can go fuck yourself," he hisses.

"That's enough!" our father speaks sternly between gritted teeth. "I'm in charge of how things are dealt with, and you need to learn to live with it."

My disdain grows stronger for the two of them every day. This is the life I was born into, according to him, and there's no way out.

He angles his head at Nick. "You'll handle the latest piece of business without any bloodshed until I tell you any differently. Do I make myself clear?"

"Crystal." Nick's jaw rocks back and forth.

"What business now?" I ask.

"None of your concern. I want you to focus on the shipping containers being delivered and dispersed properly."

"Why do his hands always stay clean and mine dirty?" Nick whines.

"Shut the hell up. You like being the cleaner, and you know it."

"That's because you think you're morally better

than me, but in reality, you don't have the guts to do my job," he sniffs, curling his upper lip.

I can't argue with him; I don't. I've done a lot of dirty things for this family, but I've never killed a man.

"He has his job, you have yours. Now stop the bullshit between the two of you. I don't want to hear it on my time." He continues to talk about a previous investigation into our family where millions of dollars were at stake, and charges were pending against all of us, and how Nick saved our necks. He likes to feed Nick's ego. I believe it's his way of controlling him.

I roll the solid block of ice around in my bourbon, tuning out his words, and briefly scan the restaurant. My gaze lands on a strikingly gorgeous woman with silky black hair sitting at a table alone. She's got long legs to die for crossed underneath her. Strands of black fall at her breast line, clinging to her white blouse that's loosely buttoned. Her eye color reminds me of the square chewy caramel candy my mother used to give me for being a good boy.

"Our reputation is at stake if we let things slide, and I'm not about to give up my power, so the two of you better damn well do your jobs," my father rants, and I have no idea what specifically he was talking about.

When her stare meets mine, I suck in my breath. At thirty-eight years old, I've had no weakness for any woman, but just looking at her raw beauty brings me to my knees. Women throw themselves at my feet because of my money, and they easily spread their legs for me. They pull out all their dirty tricks to get me in their beds. I'm the type of man who willingly accommodates them but has them removed before the sun rises. I don't claim to be a saint, and I'm not. I have the mindset that if they're willing to use me for the almighty dollar, then why shouldn't I take advantage of scratching an itch. I love sex. The dirtier, the better.

Feeling overcome with an insurmountable need to meet this gorgeous creature, I excuse myself and stride to her table. Instead of offering my hand, I comment that I haven't seen her in here before. She answers with a distant look in those caramel eyes of hers.

"Noa Sutton." She sticks out her hand and smiles, displaying dimples in both of her cheeks.

Her last name rolls around in my head. "Sutton. Any relationship to the man that used to own this joint?"

Her smile fades, and there's a slight tremble in her bottom lip. "He's my late husband."

I'd heard he was killed in a home invasion. "I'm so sorry." I can't bear the thought of touching her hand and not wanting to console her, so I shove it in my pocket. "I love The Italian Oven. It's my favorite place to eat in Manhattan. I come here at least once a month, if not more."

"I didn't catch your name." She cocks one of her dark brows.

"Ever Christianson."

"That's very unusual." Her grin is back.

"I get that a lot." I can't stop myself from smiling. I want to get to know her. "Have dinner with me," I blurt out very uncharacteristically. I'm usually the one pursued, not the other way around.

"Seems to me you already have a dinner date or two." She glances over my shoulder at my father and idiot brother.

"None as beautiful as you."

"This seat is taken," the bartender abruptly interrupts us, crossing his arms over his chest in a protective stance. His build reminds me of a bouncer, and I don't choose to get into a scuffle with him.

My gaze darts between them, and I dig my teeth into my bottom lip. "It was very nice to meet you,

Noa," I speak her name, one that I will not soon forget, as I walk backward, reluctantly returning to my dinner companions.

"I'm glad you felt the need to return. We were in the middle of discussing business," my father huffs.

No one leaves Carmine Leone waiting. Not even his sons. I didn't grow up with wealth or with the knowledge that I had a father until my mother was found facedown in our swimming pool when I was ten years old. It was ruled an accident, but I've never believed it. I lived in Florida with her, and she taught me how to swim before I could even walk. No matter how much I shouted it from the rooftops, no one believed me, and they closed her case without an investigation. Her death has always plagued me. That's when my dear old dad came into the picture and moved me to New York.

The Leone family amassed their wealth by any cutthroat means possible under the guise of being real estate developers. My father was irate when I refused to change my name from Christianson to Leone, which was my mother's maiden name. I still can feel the sting of his belt strap on my back. It was raw for days, but I refused to give in to his demands. My association with him comes with both good and bad. Money and women being the bonus. The ill deeds I do for him will be my downfall. I tell myself I'm innocent because I don't ask what's in the shipping containers or other deliveries that are made or who he's blackmailed to gain control over all the properties he owns, not to mention the deaths he's ordered to keep his power or to simply prove a point that the Leone family is not to be messed with.

I don't want to know because it would make me a sick bastard like him. Perhaps I'm fooling myself. I already am. It's a life I never wanted or asked for. I was happier being the poor white boy of a single mom. She gave me more unconditional love than I deserved. She'd hate the man I've become, and I can't say I'd blame her.

I flash a glance back over to Noa's table, and I can't stop the corner of my mouth from lifting until my father begins his rant again.

"If you want a woman, I can make one phone call and have her waiting for you at your apartment. I demand your undivided attention!" The silverware rattles when he bounces his fist on the table.

"I don't need you to get a woman for me," I quip.

"Yeah, he runs through them like water." Nick's lip snarls. "He can't find one to hold on to."

"Your wife only stays with you because of money, and you cheat on her every time the opportunity arises."

"She looks fucking good on my arm," he spats. "Don't think you're any better than me."

He's right. I'm just as big of an asshole. I crane my neck toward Noa's table, and she's leaving with the woman that runs this place. *You're better off not knowing me.*

Our father tells us what his expectations of us for the week are and the fact that he's hired a new man to help out with tough negotiations to free up some of Nick's time in order to handle the financial end of the business.

"I expect the container deliveries to be on time. You'll meet with two potential buyers and take the best deal. I've already written down the lowest number I'll accept." He hands me a folder with the names of the buyers and a number followed by lots of zeros. "And I'm confident you will bring much more than that."

"Aren't you ever curious about what's in the shipping containers?" Nick drums his fingers on the table.

"Not in the least."

"The less he knows, the better. Someone has to stay out of jail if shit hits the fan. We'll need him to bail us out. He's better off being the middleman."

The waitress comes over and tops off our drinks, and sets the bill on the table. My father pulls out a bundle of cash and hands it to her, telling her to keep the change. He always leaves a big tip, but it's only for show. Carmine Leone enjoys letting women know that he's wealthy. High-end call girls frequent his place often. I asked him once if he'd ever remarry, and he said he had one love in his life and didn't need another. He did live with a woman for a bit, and she bore him a son who she left behind when she ran away with another man.

He had a funny way of showing my mother he loved her. Their story was always a secret kept from me by both of them. Being as sweet as she was, I can only imagine my mother had no idea about the man she had married or the acts that he was capable of doing. The best thing she could've done for both of us was run, and I don't blame her one bit. I fully believe she left him to protect me from my father... and yet here I sit, working for the man who is thick as thieves with Satan himself.

As I stand to leave, Noa comes back into the

dining area with Sofia on her heels. She looks as if she's been crying, and it gut punches me. I stick around after my father and brother leave in hopes of chatting with her again. The bartender gives me a *get the hell out of here* look, and I walk out of the restaurant and lean my back against the brick building, waiting for her under an awning.

"I'll meet you at my house later," Sofia says from the doorway.

Noa fastens her jacket and steps out onto the sidewalk in the rain.

"You're going to get soaked," I say, offering her refuge under the umbrella I left outside when I went into the restaurant.

"I'm good," she utters, pulling the hood over her head.

"I don't mind sharing." A grin creeps on my face again. She seems to have some sort of effect on me.

"You don't even know what direction I'm headed." She purses her lips to keep from smiling.

"I'd be a fool not to go wherever you're going." I laugh. "Never say I'd let a beautiful woman get rained on in the streets of Manhattan."

"I'm sorry." She blinks several times. "I'm only in town for a short period of time. No sense in wasting your charm on me." She starts to walk, but I lay my hand on her elbow.

"Let me convince you to a lengthier stay."

"Look," she huffs. "I don't know you from Adam, and I've had a really long day. I'd like to get settled in for the night."

Visions of her restrained beneath me flood my mind. "Then say yes to meeting me for breakfast in the morning."

"I don't think so…"

"That's not a no." My brow raises.

"You're a man that is used to getting what he wants, aren't you?" She crosses her arms under her breasts, and it's extremely distracting.

"I can be very persistent."

"I'm afraid you're going to be disappointed then."

Her turning me down has my cock aching, and I want nothing more than to haul her against my chest and steal a kiss from her full lips. I hold out the umbrella. "At least take this so you can stay dry. You can leave it at the restaurant the next time you visit it."

She hesitantly takes it from me. "Thank you."

"You're very welcome, Noa Sutton." Her name flows off my tongue so easily.

She strolls a few feet down the sidewalk and

peers over her shoulder at me, and I know I've gotten to her. I casually wave as the rain puddles in my hair, dripping into my collar. I watch her backside as she makes it to the corner, waiting on the crosswalk. It flashes the okay signal, and all the pedestrians cross but her. She stands stock-still.

My shoes hit the wet concrete hard as I make my way to her, splashing water on my pant legs. She turns to face me when I'm a few feet away.

"Breakfast, nothing more," she states, and I see vulnerability in her eyes. "There's a diner on Thirty-Seventh Street."

"Between Seventh and Eighth. I know it very well. May I have the honor of picking you up?" I sound all gentlemanly, but I have ulterior motives that involve doing wicked things to her sexy body and skipping breakfast altogether.

"No. I'll meet you there at seven." She turns on her heels and waits for the light to change, then crosses over to the other side, never looking back again.

I tug my phone from my jacket pocket and call the diner, offering them a substantial amount of money to close it down to everyone other than the two of us, and they agree. This is the part of wealth I really enjoy.

Hustling to make it to the docks before the sun sets fully, my driver weaves through traffic and runs a few lights to get me to Red Hook Marine Terminal on the Lower East Side.

The dock employees are already working on the containers being lifted onto the awaiting ship. My father pays the captain a handsome salary to take his precious cargo where he sees fit. I count them to make sure they are all accounted for and linger at the last one, running my hand down the cold metal. "What's inside of your walls?" I whisper, then curb my curiosity, shaking my head. "I've gone this long without knowing."

The men my father spoke of show up soon after me. One is short and stocky, dressed in an expensive jogging suit that I'd bet my life has never been used for its intent, based on the sight of his protruding midsection. He has a thick gold chain dangling around his neck and large rings on his left hand. The other man is dressed to the nines in a business suit and an expensive hat with a cigar perched between his lips.

Without looking through the file, I take out the papers I know are relevant to what's in the containers. The short, stocky dude's eyes bulge. "This is some top-notch shit."

"Did you expect any differently from Carmine Leone?" I half laugh.

He makes an offer, and the other guy counters it. They go back and forth, far exceeding the amount my father demanded. I stand and wait for them to argue between the two of them before they decide to make it a partnership and split their profits. They shake hands, and we settle on a final amount. My father will be pleased.

"Write down where you want the containers shipped, and they'll leave the terminal tonight," I tell them.

Once my business is done, I climb in the back seat of my black Mercedes Benz S550 and direct my driver to take me home in Central Park South. I live in the penthouse suite in the Ritz-Carlton. Personally, I'd rather live in the countryside, but my father insists I live like a king. The only thing good about it is the view from my balcony.

As soon as the elevator stops on the top floor, I kick out of my shoes and head straight to my bar, pour a bourbon, then open up the doors to the city below me. The rain has slowed to a drizzle, and the sky is dark and gloomy, matching how I feel most of the time. Polishing off my drink, I pour another and then sit at my computer, wanting to know more about Noa Sutton.

Pictures of Noa and her husband pop up immediately. Graduated from Boston College with a journalism degree. Originally from Essex, Massachusetts, where she grew up with her parents and one sibling. "Sofia Laurent. Why is she managing the restaurant and not Noa?" I read further into the night of the home invasion. "Damn." I run my hand down the length of my face over my five o'clock shadow. "It must have been horrifying for her." It says she was hit over the head and escaped with only minor injuries. Physically perhaps, but mentally it had to have done a number on her mind.

Why do I feel an extremely unfounded need to console this woman? She has me completely perplexed, and I'm dying to touch every part of her. I rock back in my chair and latch my hands behind my head. "Hasn't she been hurt enough? She doesn't need a man like me who will only use her for my own pleasure."

Exhaling, I stand, take my glass with me, and hook the decanter with one finger as I move to the balcony. Occasional drops of rain ping my face as if they're trying to get my attention. How did I let myself get sucked into this life? I have no family other than the evil bloodline I belong to, who I'm working for. Long gone are the days I dreamed of anything for myself. The only legit thing I do is the properties I buy and sell on the side without my father's knowledge. I'm a prisoner in my own world.

3 NOA

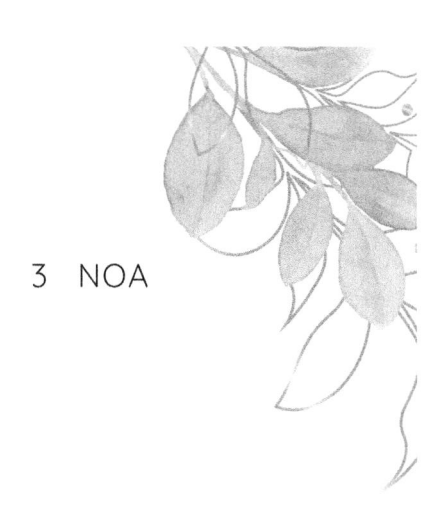

I'm exhausted, but when I cross the sidewalk and see the architect's building, I have to stop. Shaking out the umbrella, I rest it against the stuccoed wall before I open the door and take the elevator to the third floor. I'm greeted by a secretary in a tight pencil skirt with an equally snug bun on top of her head.

"I'm sorry, but the office is closed," she says, grabbing her Coach purse and slinging it over her shoulder.

I see the light on under his door. "Can you just poke your head in his office and tell him Noa Sutton is here to see him?" I point to his door.

She lets out an annoyed sound from her lips, and

her heels clack quickly on the tile floor, lightly knocking prior to opening his door.

"There's someone named Noa here to see you. I told her the office was closed, but she insisted I let you know."

"Noa!" His voice rises in excitement, and I hear his chair roll over the wood floor. Within seconds he's holding his arms out. "It's so good to see you."

I walk into his embrace. "It's been a while," I mutter.

"I'll see you tomorrow," his secretary says, raking her eyes over him like a jealous woman before she stomps out of the office.

"I see you haven't changed a bit." I laugh. "Have you ever thought about hiring a staff member you didn't want to sleep with?"

"What would be the fun in that?" He chuckles and walks me into his office, where I sink into his plush leather couch.

Kip Oliver and my husband were best friends in college, and any trouble Drake got into could always be traced back to Kip, but he truly loved him like a brother.

He joins me on the couch and props his arm over the back. "How are you?"

"I'm good. Some days." I lift a shoulder.

"You hate New York. What are you doing here, and why didn't you let me know you were coming to the city?"

"Sofia beckoned me." I sigh. "There's some business I need to handle, and she felt like she needed to see me in person."

"Anything I can help with?"

"It's financial stuff. Evidently, without my knowledge, Drake borrowed money from investors over and above the bank loan."

"Yeah." He leans forward on the couch, rubbing his hands together. "He came to me needing money the second year he opened to keep things afloat."

"Oh thank God it's you he owes money to." Relief washes over me.

"Not exactly. I was just making a name for myself, and every penny I had earned, I sank into my architectural firm. But I did introduce him to a real estate investor of sorts." He mumbles the last part.

"Of sorts? What does that mean?" The look of concern on his face is making me nervous.

He abruptly stands and paces in front of me. "I should've done more research into the company before I ever suggested he do business with them. I've had nothing but regret for recommending them to Drake."

"Why?" I reach out and touch his hand.

He sits and draws a leg up between us. "Have you ever heard of the Leone family?"

I shake my head.

"They operate under the guise of real estate investors." He runs a hand through his thick hair.

"What are they really?" My lip trembles.

"The best way I know to describe them is a mob family operating organized crime."

I hop to my feet. "This is who I owe money to?" The pitch in my voice raises several octaves.

"As long as you pay them what you owe them, there won't be an issue." He gets to his feet and braces his hands on my shoulder.

"The restaurant is doing well, but we can't come up with the amount of money they are demanding. According to the contract Drake signed, the money wouldn't be due for another five years, but there was a clause in the fine print stating they could call it due at any time they saw fit."

"Let me handle it. I'll negotiate with them. Perhaps they'll commit to monthly payments until it's paid in full."

"You really think you can negotiate with a mafia family?"

"I'll try. I got you into this mess, and I'll do my

damndest to get you out of it. I owe it to Drake. I'm so sorry. If I had known, I would have never introduced him to Nick Leone."

"I can't be angry with you. You were only trying to help my husband."

"Are you staying with Sofia while you're here?"

"Yes."

"How long will you be in town? I'd love to take the two of you out to dinner."

"I was planning on leaving tomorrow, but with this news, I need to stick around until it's worked out. I'm going to set up a meeting with them."

"Please don't. Let me try to handle it first. I don't want you any more involved with them than you already are. Give me a week."

"Alright, as long as you keep me posted."

"I will. I promise." He walks me to the door. "Have you been by the apartment?"

"No. But I've decided to sell it. I will never live there again, and it's a constant reminder of what happened the night Drake died."

"I can handle that for you, too, if you'd like."

"I need to do it by myself. Perhaps it will give me closure." I hug him.

"I'll call you, and I was serious about dinner."

"Thanks, Kip," I tell him and take the elevator to the ground floor.

The doorman at Sofia's apartment building recognizes me and lets me through the double doors and rides with me up the elevator to the fifth floor, and unlocks her door for me.

"Thank you," I say.

"You're welcome. I hope you enjoy your visit, Mrs. Sutton."

Sofia's place is modest and scantly decorated. She'd rather spend her money on clothes and a fine bottle of wine than decor. She's three years older than me but far wiser when it comes to business, graduating at the top of her class from Boston College in Hotel and Restaurant Management. Sofia introduced Drake and me during our freshmen year. She met him in one of the lecture halls and knew we'd be perfect together, and I couldn't argue with her from the first minute I laid eyes on him. He was of French and Italian descent, just like me. His skin was a beautiful shade of olive, and his hair was the blackest I'd ever seen. I found him to be very sexy and motivated. He saw an opportunity in things that others didn't, and he'd jump on it with everything he had to make it a reality. I loved that about him and the fact that he always made me laugh.

We married shortly after we graduated college, and I never regretted it for a moment. That's not to say we didn't struggle, we did, but we did it together. We were apart a lot once he bought the restaurant because he needed to be there all the time, and my job required me to travel. We never went a day without talking to one another before we went to bed. I thought we told each other everything, but apparently, I was wrong. He never let on that the restaurant was in any kind of financial trouble. I trusted him fully with everything. There was a moment I was concerned when he wanted to hire my sister as the manager. Not because she wasn't totally qualified, I just was concerned about the two of them working together. What if they didn't end up getting along or didn't see eye to eye? I didn't want it to affect our relationship. That fear subsided quickly. She was the perfect match for his personality. He adored her, and she him.

Opening the door to her guest room, I see my suitcase the airline delivered and unzip it, taking out a pair of pajamas. Stepping into the bathroom, I slide the shower door open and turn on the hot water. Peeling out of my clothes, I let the water soak away my day, recalling my conversation with Kip and then to the handsome stranger in the restaurant. Why did

I agree to have breakfast with him? Because he was entrancing? Perhaps I need a fling to help me move on. His confidence was sexy, and it's been a really long time since I've had sex. In fact, Drake was the only man I'd ever slept with, and I thought he'd be my one and only.

"Are you in here? I hear the shower running," Sofia's voice rings out.

"You're home," I say, peeking through the door.

"I brought you a bottle of wine. I figured you could use it. Did you go by the apartment?"

"No. I'll face that one tomorrow. I did stop by and see Kip and told him about the loan. You won't believe who the money is owed to."

"Who?" She leans against the sink.

"Do you know who the Leone family is?"

"Sounds familiar."

"They are a mob family. Kip is the one that introduced them. He had no idea at the time what he'd gotten Drake into."

"You're kidding me," she gasps. "That's who's calling in the loan?" She opens the shower door.

I snag a towel from a hook and turn off the water. "Kip is going to try and negotiate a deal with them so that we can pay them back each month."

"Do you think that's going to work? A family like the Leones don't usually change their minds."

I step out of the shower, and she hands me a glass filled to the brim with wine. "We're going to find out."

"Does that mean you're staying for a bit?"

"Yes. I'm not leaving you to deal with it. If he can't work something out, I'll be forced to sell the restaurant."

"Maybe I could take out a personal loan and buy it myself. I love The Italian Oven, and I'd hate for anyone else to own it."

"And I'd love for it to be yours."

"I'll contact my bank and see what they'd be willing to loan me. I've saved a lot of money, and I'm sure between the two, I can afford it. Why didn't I think of this earlier? It will give you the money you need to pay off the debt, and you'll still be able to keep a piece of Drake."

I press my lips to the glass, sipping the wine. "This is just what I needed to relax. It's been a really long day, and I want nothing more than to lay my head on a pillow."

"I was hoping we could stay up late and catch up."

After drying, I slip on my pajamas, and she follows me out of the bathroom. "Can I take a rain check until tomorrow?" I ask through a wide yawn and stretch my arms.

"You never were one to stay up late," she snorts. "I've always been the night owl. How did sisters get to be so different?"

"Because you were always more of a handful than me." I laugh. "Mom and Dad tried to rein you in, but you were their wild child."

"You're welcome because it took the attention off of you, and I don't think you could complain because you were Daddy's favorite."

"You know that's not true. He adores you."

"Now, perhaps, but you had him wrapped around your little finger. All you had to do was bat your caramel eyes that matched his, and he'd hand you his credit card."

"He did spoil me," I snicker.

"I couldn't bring home anyone that he approved of, and the minute he met Drake, he fell in love with him as much as you did."

"You're the one that introduced us. Why didn't you ever date him?"

"He was handsome and all, but I knew the second I met him he was meant for you and no one else."

I plop on the edge of the bed. "I miss him."

She sits beside me, wrapping her arm around my

shoulder. "I know you do. So do I. And as much as I know you loved him, it's time to move on. He'd want you to find someone else and be happy."

"I'd settle for a night of hot sex." I smirk.

"That would be a start," she murmurs.

I don't share with her that I'm having breakfast with a complete stranger in the morning because it will probably turn out to be nothing. I'll chicken out with thoughts of Drake scrambling in my head.

She stands, and I crawl under the covers. "I'm shorthanded in the afternoon behind the bar. What do you say to helping out like you used to?"

"I think it might be fun."

"Good, I'll tell Bruno you'll be there by two. He's taking Gia to her first OB appointment."

"She's pregnant?" I yip, filled with warmth for the two of them.

"Yes, and they are so excited. He's going to be a great dad."

"Thank you for handling things for me when I couldn't." I curl on my side.

She walks to the door and flips off the light. "Get some rest. I'll be gone before you wake up."

"Good night."

4 NOA

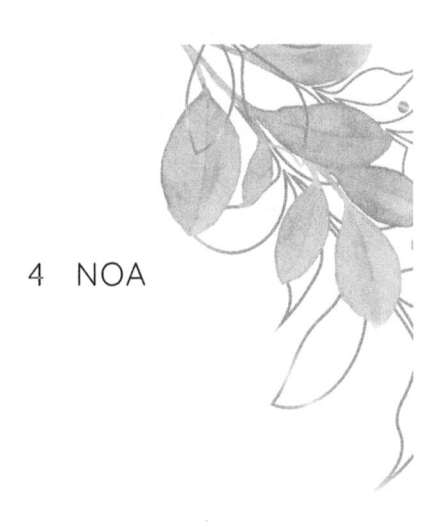

What was I thinking? Why did I agree to meet him, and why didn't I just not show up? I ask myself all these things entering the empty, greasy diner. And for heaven's sake, why did I choose this place? Drake and I used to eat here on Sunday mornings when I was in town. He'd get out of bed early and go to the restaurant, get things started, and then come here to have breakfast with me. I cherished our Sundays together. We'd sit across from one another, hold hands and talk about anything and everything under the sun and what our future looked like together.

"I can't do this," I mumble and spin on my heels, only to find myself plowing into someone's chest.

"Leaving so soon?" Ever is looking down on me,

and I have to catch my breath from staring into his emerald eyes.

"The place is empty. I thought it was closed," I lie, wanting an excuse to leave.

He takes my elbow and guides me to a booth. "It's empty because that's the way I wanted it," he says.

"Do you always get what you want?" I frown at him from my seat, and he slides in the other side of the booth.

"Most of the time, when it comes to things money can buy." He eases one shoulder higher than the other.

I study him for a long moment. He's by far the most captivatingly handsome man I've ever met. His polished suit is gone, and he's rocking a gray-blue pullover, a pair of jeans, and he doesn't appear to have shaved this morning. The sight of him makes my toes curl.

He shoots me a wickedly sexy, lopsided grin like he's keenly aware of me checking him out. "You look radiant," he states.

I mash my lips together and rub my hands down my skinny jean-clad thighs. "What do you want from me?"

"Breakfast with you to start." He waves the lone

waitress over to our table. "I'll have a black cup of coffee."

"And you, miss?" she asks.

"I thought you wanted something to eat?"

"Coffee is my choice of breakfast foods."

I typically only have a piece of avocado toast, but if breakfast with me is what he wants, then that's what he's going to get. "I'll have three eggs over medium, hash browns, bacon, rye toast, and a glass of orange juice with ice."

She scribbles on her pad of paper. "Anything else?"

"A stack of pancakes, oh, and coffee loaded with cream and sugar."

The waitress walks away, and he bursts out laughing. "There is no way you can eat that much food."

Challenge taken, and I'm sure I'm going to pay for it later. "Watch me."

He rubs his hands together. "I can hardly wait to see this. Are you going to use this opportunity to critique their food?"

I bite the corner of my mouth. "You googled me."

"I did."

"For your information, I've eaten here many

times before, and I don't rate the food of places I frequent."

He rests back against the booth. "Including The Italian Oven? I believe I read an article about you raving over the stuffed mushrooms that you were devouring yesterday."

"You were watching me?"

"As you were me."

He's right. I was, but I want to deny it.

"I'd have to be blind not to notice a woman like you."

"A woman like me," I repeat his words back to him. In my mind, I was off-kilter yesterday being back in Manhattan, overwhelmed with sorrow. What the heck could he have seen in me other than a mess? Perhaps the damsel in distress look appeals to him.

"When you reappeared with your sister, you'd been crying." It's a statement, not a question.

"I haven't been back in the restaurant since I left Manhattan. There was a picture of my husband and me on his…her office wall." Why do I feel the need to explain myself to him?

"That must have been very difficult. I'm sorry for your loss." A genuine expression of sadness fills the crevices of his eyes. "I recall reading an article about his death. How long ago was it?"

"Two years."

The waitress brings our drinks to the table. "Your food will be out shortly," she states and returns to the kitchen.

"Did they ever catch his killers?"

"No." I drop my gaze to my lap.

"Are you here on business or pleasure?" His tone changes to something much lighter.

"Business, and I'll be returning to Essex as soon as it's finished. I'm sure you searched where I was from too." I look him point-blank in the eyes.

"Do you not like Manhattan?"

"There are a lot of bad memories here. Some good ones, too, but the bad outweighs the good."

"I'd like to alter that for you."

The waitress lays a plate of food in front of me. I don't think I can eat it, but I force myself to pick up my fork and push it around my plate. "You're obviously a very handsome, well-to-do man, and you could entertain a multitude of women. So, I'll ask you again, what do you want from me?"

"You intrigue me. You're sad, but there's an underlying fervor for life dying to get out of you. I see it in the way you move."

"And you think you can draw that out of me?" I snort.

"I could at least make you forget your sadness for a bit."

"Really? How would you go about doing that?" I wipe my mouth with the paper napkin and drum my fingernails on the laminate table.

He eases his arm across the table and lays his hand on mine to stop the drumming. "Spend the day with me." There's so much heat he's putting off between us that I have to adjust in my seat and press my thighs together to dull an unnerving ache.

"I only agreed to breakfast. I have some things I need to handle while I'm in the city."

"Let me tag along. Maybe I could help with those said things."

"You're a complete stranger to me, and I can't believe I agreed to this in the first place." I snatch the fork from his hand, ticked at myself for wanting the possibility of being held in a stranger's arms, even if only for a night.

"Are you angry at me or those eggs you're mutilating?" He laughs.

Inhaling, I calm my nerves, take a sip of my juice, and wipe the corner of my mouth again. "Who are you, Ever Christianson? My friend, the bartender, made it very clear that I needed to stay away from you. Who were those men you were having dinner with last night?"

He shifts in the booth. "I'm a man who knows what he likes when he sees it, and I agree with your friend. You do need to stay away from the man you saw last night. He's cutthroat, but the man you're sitting across from now is someone who wants to be different. Who wants more out of life than what money can buy him."

"You've decided that thing you want is me?" I press a finger to the base of my throat.

"For some inexplicable reason…yes." He stares at me with those emerald greens, and I swear they see right through me as to how much I'm turned on by him.

This complete stranger stirs up emotions I didn't know I still had in me, and I don't know what to do with them. If he senses them, he'll devour me, and I'll let him. His sizzling sex appeal is more than my starving libido can bear. "You'll have to find another woman." I slide out of the booth. "I'm afraid I can't help you. Thank you for breakfast." I all but run out of the diner to get away from him.

I make it to within steps of my sister's car I borrowed before his hand grasps my shoulder and spins me to face him. He presses his body against mine, trapping me between the car and his chest. "Please don't go," he rasps next to my ear. "Not without letting me kiss you. I'm dying to know what you taste like."

"Eggs," I stammer, squeezing my eyes closed because if I look at his lips, I know I'll want the same thing.

"When's the last time you've been so thoroughly kissed by someone that it brought you nothing but an aching pleasure with a promise of so much more?" He whispers his question.

His voice is tantalizing and sexy. I shake my head, searching in my mind for the last kiss I shared with Drake. It was the night he died. I surprised him at our apartment, not telling him I'd be home. At first, he acted a little out of sorts, and over our dinner, he said he had something he wanted to tell me, but I lured him into our bed with the vow he could tell me tomorrow, which never came for him.

"Please, don't." My tone is hushed but filled with wanting.

He takes a step back, putting some space between us. "The next time we find ourselves in this type of situation, you'll have to ask me to kiss you."

"There won't be a next time." I swallow hard, ignoring how soaked my panties are right now.

He shoves his hands in his pockets and grins. "I'll see you around, Noa Sutton."

My fingers tremble, unlocking the car. I get behind the wheel and watch him climb into the back seat of his vehicle. His windows are so black that I can't see his silhouette once he's inside. Gray smoke blows from his tailpipe as his driver pulls out into traffic.

Part of me wants to chase him down, crawl in the back seat with him, and take the kiss he was offering. The sensible part of me wins out and drives through the streets of Manhattan until I make it to my destination. I use my ID to open the gates to the parking garage and lose track of time as to how long I've been sitting in my car, trying to convince myself to go inside. My phone ringing jars me.

"Hey," I say to Sofia.

"I wanted to make sure you got out of bed. I know how depressing this city is for you."

"Yeah, I'm good." I swallow to bring moisture back into my mouth. "I'm in the parking garage to the apartment."

"Oh, sweetie, why don't you put it off and wait

until I can go with you? I'll rearrange my schedule, and we can do it together tomorrow."

"I appreciate it, but it's something I need to do alone. It's time."

"Are you sure?"

"Yes." My lip quivers in uncertainty.

"Alright. I'll see you this afternoon."

Bravely, I get out of the car and head for the elevator. Once I make it to the sixth floor, I stand in front of the door with the keys tucked in my hand. "You have to do this," I utter as a tear slips in my mouth.

The apartment we owned is the only one on the sixth floor, and it's two stories tall. Drake fell in love with this place the moment he saw it. I wanted something quaint on the outskirts of Manhattan, but he insisted on being downtown near the restaurant. He didn't own a car, so it was perfectly within walking distance for him. I reluctantly gave in, and I never quite felt like the place was mine. He decorated how he saw fit and was very comfortable with it. I only loved it because he did.

Stepping inside, the closed-up stench hits me in the face. It always smelled of his cologne and whatever wine he'd brought home for me to try. I was his guinea pig. If I approved of the wine, he sold it at the restaurant.

The white walls seem grayer, and the oak floors have lost their luster. The living room boasts high ceilings and flows into the kitchen in one wide open space. The one thing I did always like was the tall windows lining the room, letting in the light. Glass doors open to a painted concrete patio area overlooking the city. The plants that were left behind are shriveled in their decorative pots.

My heart starts racing the moment I lay my foot on the first marble stair. Gripping the metal handrail, I steady my uneasiness and slowly take the stairs one step at a time. I fall to my knees when I reach the landing, and I'm thrust back into that horrible night. This is where I found Drake gasping for air with blood spilling from the corner of his mouth. I'd been hit in the head with the butt of a gun and was frantic when I woke up, screaming Drake's name.

I cradled him in my arms, begging him not to leave me. His eyes were glazed over and already lacking signs of life as I held him, screaming with every ounce of breath in my lungs for someone to help us. No one heard my agonizing cries, and he took his last breath as I kissed his face. Scrambling to my phone, I called 911 and pounded on his chest, pleading with him to wake up until the police arrived. It was too late, Drake was gone, and I was all alone.

Wiping tear after tear as if it was yesterday, I get to my feet like a zombie and enter the bedroom we shared. Sofia had the place cleaned spotless after the funeral, and it appears exactly how I remember it. Our white down comforter looks inviting on the bed, with soft pillows in shades of blue nestled against the headboard.

I sit on the edge and run my hand over the comforter in hopes of feeling Drake's presence. Curling on my side, I lay my head on his pillow, and the faint scent of him still remains.

"I miss you so much," I sniff. "I wish every day you were still here." I cry for a long moment before I sit tall. Opening his side table, I pick up a few of his personal items, clutching them to my chest. Pulling the drawer open wider, I see a notebook in the very back. It never dawned on me when he was alive to open this drawer. I had no need; it was his.

Taking it out, I thumb through the first couple of pages listing dates and times we'd spent together. The time grows further and further apart. It switches to his business and the struggles I never knew he was having with it. Then he talks about being lonely in a busy world, missing his wife, and that he'd never ask me to give up my dream job, but he yearned for me to be with him every day.

My heart lurches. I so wish he would've told me how he felt. Outwardly, he was so supportive of my dreams. Once I clear the lump in my throat, I read more and find myself gasping. He talks about a woman who he can't stop thinking about and has fought his feelings for as long as he can, but he has to end it before he does any more damage. *I need to tell her my secret before she finds out.*

I can't believe the words I'm reading. "He had an affair," I gulp. Skimming the pages, I search for a name or any indication of who she was.

"Did Sofia know? Was he going to end things with me or the other woman? Was that his secret, or was there more?" I ask out loud in an empty room, feeling as if I'm losing my mind.

In the next section, he describes ending his relationship with her because of his profound guilt. "You should've felt guilty!" I scream as loud as I did the night I was calling for help to save him.

Falling back on the bed, I wail. It's bad enough I lost him, but to find out I had already lost him to another woman is even more painful than I thought possible. I lie crying until my eyes are swollen, and there are no more tears to be shed.

"It was my fault. I should've been here with my husband, not traveling around the country...for what? To critique food? There should've been nothing more important than my marriage. Nothing."

When I finally get to my feet, I take the notebook with me, lock the place up and drive mindlessly to the restaurant, parking in the owner's dedicated spot.

Looking into the rearview mirror, I wipe the streaks of mascara from my cheeks and straighten my messy hair. Snatching my purse, and the notebook, I stride inside and march over to Sofia, who is greeting a couple at a table.

"Did you know about this?" I snarl, holding the book out.

"Excuse me," she says to the couple and pulls me aside. "Did I know about what, and can we discuss whatever has gotten you upset in a calmer voice?" She ushers me into her office.

"Drake was having an affair!" I throw the notebook on her desk.

"What are you talking about?"

"It's all in there. Who was she?" I snap.

"I…I don't know. Drake loved you. There must be some mistake. Where did you get this?" She picks it up.

"In his nightstand. It's in his own handwriting, so there's no misunderstanding his words. It had to be someone he met here." I stab my finger into her desk.

She tosses it aside and hugs me. "I'm so sorry. This has to be devastating to you."

"I trusted him." I sob uncontrollably on her shoulder.

"We all did."

"What am I going to do?"

"There is nothing you can do. He's gone, and at this point, it really doesn't matter who she was."

"I feel like I've been skewered in the heart. I should've never come back here."

"You look at me." She places her hands on either side of my face. "This is even more of a reason for you to get your life back on track. Please don't let this take the last bit of spark you have."

"I just want to go home," I whine.

"This is one of those times in life our father would tell you to put your big girl panties on and suck it up. You can't leave until we've settled the issues with the restaurant. I know how painful this is, but perhaps it's the push you need."

"Finding out my husband, who I thought hung the moon, had an affair!"

"Yes, because it's pissing you off. You need to be angry and then forgive him."

"Oh, I'm angry, alright!" I wave my hands. "Forgiveness is not even in the realm of what I'm thinking!"

"Good. I'm mad for you, but get it all out!"

I fall into a chair like the wind has been taken from my sail. "The bad part is that I can't blame him. I was hardly ever around, chasing some meaningless dream."

She stands me up and shakes my shoulders. "I'm not going to let you blame yourself for your husband's affair. He should have talked to you and told you how lonely he was feeling instead of screwing around."

"I was feeling the same way."

"But you didn't act on it. Did you?" She raises a brow.

"No. The thought never even crossed my mind. I adored my husband, and I thought we were a team, both living out our dreams, supporting one another. Now that he's gone, I wish I would've done things differently. If we weren't so focused on our careers, we would've had children by now, and I wouldn't be completely alone."

"You're not alone. You can stay with me as long as you want to."

"I'm sorry to interrupt," Bruno says hesitantly from the doorway, "but I really need to leave."

I lick my lips and wipe my shoulder over my cheeks. "I understand congratulations are in order." I walk over to Bruno, hugging him. "I'm so happy for you."

"Are you okay?"

"I will be. Nothing for you to worry about. Go take care of your wife." I plaster on one of my perfectly perfected fake smiles.

"Thanks. I'll be back in a couple of hours."

"Take your time," Sofia assures him. "Us Laurant sisters have it covered."

5 EVER

"Turn around," I order my driver. "I want you to follow her. Not too close because I don't want her to see us."

"Yes, sir," Luca says, swerving the car with a hard right, then does a U-turn in the middle of the street in Manhattan with horns blaring.

"Great way to not draw attention," I snap, then tug my ringing phone from my jeans. "I'll be there in an hour," I bark at my father.

"You should've been here an hour ago. How did the deal go down?"

"Far better than you had planned."

"Good. That's why you're in the job you're in. Quit gallivanting and get your ass to the office. We have business to discuss." He hangs up.

"Do you want me to turn around again?" Luca asks, peering in the rearview mirror.

"No. Keep on track to follow the girl."

"Who is she, sir?"

Luca has been my driver since I was eighteen years old, and I consider him a friend, and he knows me very well.

"Someone I'd like to encounter without my father and brother being involved." I cut my gaze to him.

"I understand, sir."

He keeps a block between her car and ours until she pulls up to a gated garage entrance to a six-story brownstone. "I don't have access to the garage, sir," he says.

"Pull over, and I'll get out. Wait right here for me," I say, kicking open the door. Crossing the street to the entrance, there's a call button box with names listed on it. "Sutton," I mumble, reading through them. "Sixth floor."

I wait patiently for someone to leave the building, and I slip inside like I belong. Instead of using the elevator, I take the stairs until I reach the top. Cracking open the solid door, I peek inside. Keys are dangling from the doorknob of the number matching the Sutton name. Softly tiptoeing inside, I search for any sign of Noa. She's at the top of the stairs getting to her feet, and she disappears into another room.

"This was their apartment?" I whisper my question, thinking about how masculine the place looks. More like my bachelor pad than a man living with his wife. Taking in the pictures on the wall, they appeared to be happy. She's smiling at him, and he's grinning at the camera. It's a history of all the places they'd experienced together.

The sound of weeping has me quietly padding up the marble staircase. Her cries grow louder and louder the nearer I get to the top landing. I peek inside a room, and she's curled in a ball clutching a notebook. Every part of me wants to go to her and hold her to ease the pain. I refrain, knowing I'd frighten her. What is it about this woman that makes me want to hold her so badly? Outwardly, she's strong yet so vulnerable. I know if it were me and someone brutally murdered the person I loved, that's when my father's side would come out. I'd have no problem with the old adage an eye for an eye.

Her voice rings out when the crying stops. *"It was my fault. I should've been here with my husband, not traveling around the country...for what? To critique food?*

There should've been nothing more important than my marriage. Nothing."

She blames herself as if she could've prevented it. When her feet hit the floor, I scamper down the stairs and back to my awaiting car. "Drive," I demand.

This woman is all sorts of screwed up, and I need to get her out of my head. Using her would only cause more pain. She's too broken. Yet, I can't stop thinking about her and the need to feel her body beneath mine. Bringing her into my lion's den will only cause more damage. My obsession with this woman has to stop.

Luca drops me off at the front door of our building, and I ride the elevator to the third floor and go directly into my father's office. "Here," I say, handing him a briefcase full of cash. "The other half was wired into one of your offshore funds."

"Good. They'll be another shipment of cargo by the weekend."

I take a seat on his expensive Italian leather couch. "What business did you want to discuss?"

"I need you to go down to the waterfront and collect monies owed to me by one of our tenants."

"That's Nick's job, not mine."

"You'll do what you're told," he snarls.

"I'm not your errand boy anymore. As a matter of fact, I quit." I stand.

His chair squeaks when he rests back. "We've had this discussion multiple times. You can't leave the family business." His brows draw together, forming an angry arrow between his eyes.

"I want to be a legit businessman, and as long as I'm working for you, that's not going to happen. There's nothing for you to threaten me with. I have no family, no life outside of this place."

"Your mother raised you to be weak! I thought I had beaten that out of you as a kid!" He slams his hand on the desk.

"She's the only kindness I remember, and she wanted more for me than this life. It's the reason she ran as far away from you as she could!" I don't know this for a fact. I can only surmise. She never told me anything about him.

"As much as I loved your mother, she became an issue. If she hadn't left me, she would've gotten us all killed. She was lucky to live as long as she did after stealing my son."

All the air is sucked out of my lungs, and my chest burns with the realization that, in all likelihood, he had her killed. He'd never admit it, but I'll be damned if I don't find a way to prove it. "I'm done, and I'm washing my hands of the Leone name."

"Think what you will, but you'll never be anything without me. I'll ruin your reputation, and you'll beg me to take you back." I head for the door with my fists clasped at my side. "I'll take everything from you, including anyone you love."

I wheel around. "You sorry son of a…" I race toward him, but his bodyguard slams me against the wall, and kidney punches me.

"Don't make me kill you," he growls.

"Let him go. He'll come groveling back," my father calls him off.

I grind my teeth, grimacing at the sharp pain in my back.

Nick saunters into the office after hearing the commotion. "What's he done this time?" He grins las if it gives him great pleasure for our father to be angry with me.

"Why do you let him treat you like a dog?" I snarl, aiming a finger at Nick.

"This dog, as you put it, is rich." He spits out the word rich. "Why would I want to work for anyone else?"

"Money isn't everything," I seethe.

"I guess you're about to find out," my father says. "Empty out his bank account," he orders.

He tried that once before, but I changed everything over, so there's no way he can access it anymore. There's money in one account that I left, so he'd think he'd taken everything from me. It's a couple million, but small change compared to what I actually have skimmed out of it. He's the reason I moved to the Ritz-Carlton, so he'd have no ownership of any property I own.

I shrug my shirt in place. "Empty it. I don't care."

"If you even think about going to the authorities, you'll be dragged down with us. Claiming your hands are clean isn't going to help you when I have the records to prove otherwise."

My jaw twitches. "I don't plan on ratting you out, I just want to be left the hell alone and my name erased from any involvement with this family!"

"When you do come crawling back, there'll be a price to pay," my father hollers as I storm out.

I make it to the car as Luca hangs up the phone. "Let me guess, that was my old man calling to fire you as my driver."

He grins. "Yep."

"Don't worry. You'll always have a job with me."

"I never liked the old bastard anyway," he says,

shoving the gear into drive. "Where do you want to go?"

"The Italian Oven." Why? Because I need to see her beautiful face. Lion's den or not.

Traffic is heavy, and Luca reroutes us through it to get me there sooner. I'm antsy as hell, and he knows it. He comes to a rolling stop, and I jump out of the vehicle and stride to the entrance of the restaurant. Taking a deep breath in, I'm hoping like hell she's inside.

Scanning the room, I see her behind the bar, tending to customers. Her hair is scooped up in a bun, and there are no remnants of the tears she was shedding earlier. I take a seat on the only open stool at the end of the bar and wait for her to see me.

"I thought you said you only came here once a month or so." She places a square napkin with the restaurant's logo on it in front of me. "What would you like to drink."

"I can't seem to stay away from you." It's the most honest thing I've ever said to a woman. "Bourbon." I point to the bottle.

"You alright?" she asks, filling a glass half full of the brown liquid.

"Rough day." I grip the glass, gulping it down. "A block of ice and keep the bottle handy," I tell her.

"Sounds like you and I had similar days." Her eyes fill with compassion.

I want to tell her I know and how sorry I am that she's hurting. "Would you like to talk about it?"

She half grins. "I'm a little busy at the moment."

"What time will you be done?"

She glances at her watch. "I promised to help out for a couple of hours."

"Do you mind if I sit here until you're done?" How did I get to the point where I'm waiting on a woman?

"Suit yourself. I'll leave your tab open and the bottle right here." She sets it next to my glass.

I watch her interact with people. She's good at putting on a happy face, and they like her. Especially the men. I find myself completely jealous when they flirt with her. She laughs easily and has no trouble putting them in their place when they get out of line.

Every time she pushes a strand of hair around her ear and her hand lingers on her neck, my cock twitches. My lips long to kiss a trail down her delicate skin to her breasts, where I know I'll find taut nipples.

My phone that I set on the bar vibrates on the polished wood. My father's face flashes on the screen, and I turn it off. I can't believe all these years,

I never put two and two together concerning my mother's death. After his rant today, I'm sure of it. I just need to prove it.

"Would you prefer a different brand of bourbon?" she asks, picking up the bottle that I haven't touched since she left it.

"No. This one's fine."

She leans on the counter, and her top gives me a view of the curve of her breasts. "Have you eaten? I mean, more than coffee?" The corner of her lip curls upward.

"I have not," I admit with a chuckle.

"How about I order you a few of my favorite things?" Her tongue lands between her lips, and I'm dying to kiss her.

"I'd like that, but only if you'll join me."

"Will appetizers hold you over until I get off?"

Her idea of getting off and mine are worlds apart. "Stuffed mushrooms?" My suggestive gaze dips to her breasts, and she stands tall.

"Yes, to the mushrooms." Her cheeks turn the fleshy color of grapefruit.

She continues to wait on people, but every now and then, I see her glance in my direction. I'm disappointed when a runner brings out my appetizer and not Noa.

I take my time enjoying them, and she steals one out of my hand right before I pop it into my mouth. "Hey!" I laugh.

"You're taking way too long to eat these babies." She licks her fingertips, and I nearly come in my jeans.

"I was hoping you'd join me soon."

The regular bartender opens up the half door and steps up next to her. "I'm back." He scowls at me.

"Everything go okay?" Noa asks, touching his forearm.

"Yes." He smiles briefly at her before he glares at me again. He tugs her aside, and I can only imagine he's reminding her that I'm a dangerous man.

She says something to him, then steps on her tiptoes, kissing him on the cheek. "The bar is all yours now. I'm starving."

She pushes up the door and grabs my plate of mushrooms, leading me to an empty table. "I'll be right back," she says and disappears into the kitchen area. When she returns, she's carrying two glasses and a bottle of wine. "I took the liberty of ordering our food."

"I take it your friend was none too happy that you were speaking to me." I nudge my head toward the bar.

"Bruno? He'll get over it. He's overly protective of me. He and my husband were good friends."

"When I left you this morning, you dismissed me. Did something happen to change your mind?"

"Let's just say I'm tired of living in the past." She clinks her glass to mine. "I'd like to enjoy my evening with someone who doesn't know me very well. Only what you've googled." She smirks.

I want to ask her why she feels guilty about her husband, but I sense she needs to steer away from any conversation involving him. "Tell me about this job of yours. How do you stay so lean and eat so much food?"

"The secret is only a taste. If I ate everything that was piled on my plate, I'd be as big as a house."

"I thought you were going to eat a horse this morning." I chuckle, and she snorts and covers her mouth in embarrassment.

"Sorry." Her cheeks turn pink.

"Don't be. I find it charming."

She sits back and taps her nails on her glass. "Ever Christianson. I've never heard your first name before. Is it a family name?"

"I honestly don't know. I think my mother just enjoyed saying the word. You know, like…don't ever be rude. Don't ever break a girl's heart. Don't ever do that." I use my hands for emphasis, and she snorts again.

"Never ever say never," she adds with a twinkle in her eye.

"She was a great mother." My voice drops.

"Was? I'm so sorry."

"She died when I was ten years old." *Murdered is more like it.*

"How terrible." She covers her mouth with her hand.

"It was tragic and changed my world forever." I've never talked about my mother openly to anyone, but gazing into her eyes, I know she'll understand my pain.

She reaches over and lays her hand on mine. "So you were left to be raised by your father? Did you have any siblings?"

I clear the lump in my throat. "No to both of those questions. It was just the two of us living on the coast of Florida."

"What happened to you after she died?"

My life became hell. "How about you tell me more about Essex. I have to admit, I've never been there."

"It's a beautiful town, and there's nowhere else I would've chosen to grow up. My mother is a retired schoolteacher, and my father worked for the local news as a weatherman."

"I know Sofia is your sister, any other siblings?"

Our food is delivered to our table, and she waits to respond. "Just the two of us. She's three years older than me, and we've always been close."

"Sounds like the perfect family."

"Pretty close, but we had our ups and downs like any other family." She tucks her napkin in her lap.

What I would've given to have anything close to perfect. "Where did you meet your husband?" For a moment, I think I've lost her when her smile slips, but she recovers quickly.

"Actually, Sofia introduced us our freshmen year of college, and we tied the knot as soon as we graduated."

I take a bite of lasagna. "This is good."

"It was Drake's grandmother's recipe." She beams with pride.

"How did you end up in New York?"

"It was Drake's dream to own a restaurant in downtown Manhattan."

"He has good taste in many things." I sweep an appreciative gaze over her. "This is a sweet piece of property. He must have leveraged everything he had and then some to get it. I know plenty of investors who would sell their souls to purchase this place."

"Really? Because I might be in the market to sell it." That is, if Sofia isn't able to purchase it, but he doesn't need to know of that possibility.

"Why would you want to? You've got to be making a ton of money from it, and your sister would be out of a job."

"Whoever would purchase the place would be stupid not to keep her on as the manager. She's very good at her job. Drake knew it. That's why he hired her."

"You didn't have any interest in managing it after he died?"

She exhales. "No. I lost enthusiasm in a lot of things, but running a restaurant was not something I actively wanted to undertake. It was his baby, not mine."

"Still, the money has to be flowing." I'm really good at reading body language, and when her eyes narrow and her cheek dips inward from biting it, I know she's hiding something.

"Money isn't everything," she finally says.

"Funny, I was just telling that to someone earlier today." I chuckle.

6 NOA

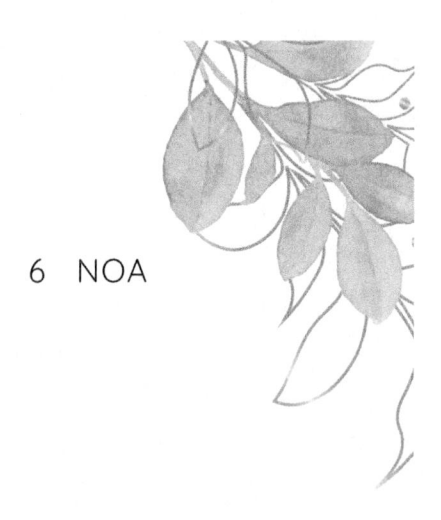

He seems completely charming. I'll have to delve deeper into a discussion with Bruno as to why he feels so strongly that I need to keep my distance from Ever.

"You have a swanky car and a driver. I doubt money has ever been an issue for you."

"True, but I'd give it all up in a heartbeat to be my own man."

"You're not your own man?" I raise a quizzical brow. Who owns him?

"That's a story for another day. How about more of this delicious wine?" He fills my glass to the rim.

"You're good at not answering questions, aren't you?"

"Mmmm-hmmm." He grins, lifting the corner of

his mouth, and it's the first time I've noticed a deep-seated dimple on his cheek. "But I have a question for you."

"I may take a cue from your playbook and not answer," I tease.

"Why did you say yes to breakfast with me?"

I straighten my spine and blow out a long breath. "Honestly, I don't know."

"Are you glad you did?"

"I'm getting there." I wink.

"Have you dated much since your husband died?"

"Not once. No one has intrigued me enough."

"Until me." He licks his lips, and I want to explore them with my tongue. Either that or it's the wine doing my thinking for me.

"Yes." It's a hard admission because some small part of me feels like this is cheating on Drake…in his restaurant. I sweep my gaze around the room, wondering if the woman he slept with is here. *Does she know me? Did she even know he was married? Was she in love with him?*

"Where'd you go?" Ever scoots his chair closer to mine so that our thighs are touching.

"Sorry, I was…never mind. Do you want to get out of here?"

"I'll take you anywhere you'd like to go."

"How about your place?"

"Do you have any idea what you'd be walking into?" His voice is breathy and warm on my cheek.

"Something very tempting…but temporary." I stare into his alluring eyes.

"As long as you understand that, then I'd be obliged to take you home."

I combat the dryness in my throat by swallowing hard and nodding. It must be the wine, or my libido run amuck, or just the fact that I find him utterly handsome and charming. A one-night stand is all I need to get him out of my system.

He tosses cash on the table.

"It's on the house," I say.

He grins and leaves the money. Taking my hand, Ever walks me out to his car and opens the back door.

"Do you mind if I run by my sister's and change clothes first?"

"You won't need clothes for what you're going to be partaking in." His fingers on my lower back already have me overheating.

I climb in and slide to the far side. Once he's inside, he reaches across my legs and drags me closer to him. "Luca, this is Noa Sutton."

"Nice to meet you, Ms. Sutton."

"Noa, please."

"Where will I be taking the two of you?" Luca asks, peering in the rearview mirror.

"To my place," Ever tells him, then pushes a button, raising a dark glass between them.

"A girl could get used to having a driver. I abhor the subway."

He clasps my hand and lightly rubs his thumb on the back of mine. "No matter what happens between us, my driver will always be at your disposal. Give me your phone."

I dig it out of my bag and place it in the palm of his outstretched hand. He taps in a phone number. "He'll be instructed to take your calls."

"You don't have to do that."

"No, I don't, but it's done." He gives it back to me.

We sit in awkward silence until Luca drives up to the hotel. "You live in the Ritz-Carlton?" I gaze out the window at the welcoming sign.

"The penthouse," he says.

Luca steps out, opens my door, and takes my hand again.

"Go ahead inside and wait for me. I have something I need to discuss with Luca," Ever says, coming around to my side of the vehicle.

The grand doors are held open by a man dressed

in a black suit with gold fringe. Once I'm in the lobby, I almost falter at its beauty. It's enormous, with white walls shimmering up to the ceiling. The lights cast diamond shards across the marble floor from the chandelier. A green-jacketed young porter approaches me.

"Do you have any luggage I can handle for you?" he asks, looking around at the ground around my feet.

"She's with me." Ever's deep voice comes up behind me.

"Sorry, Mr. Christianson. I didn't know." The young man tips his head at him.

Ever's hand returns to my lower back, and he escorts me to the cherry-finished doors of the elevator and takes out a key card. When the door opens, another porter holds back a couple wanting to enter with us. Ever flashes his card in front of the computer display, and the elevator takes us to the top floor.

"They treat you like royalty," I say, stepping into his world.

"Make yourself at home while I fix us a drink and turn on some music."

"I'll take a glass of water. I've already had enough wine." I lay my purse on the table by the door and head straight for his balcony. "What a view of the city!" I holler.

He joins me with two bottles of water. "It's the best thing about this place."

"What? No bourbon for you?"

"I don't want anything to dull my senses." His look is scorching.

Can I really do this with him? "Dance with me," I say.

"Gladly," he responds, setting the water bottles on the glass table and holding out his palm.

Placing my hand in his and the other on his shoulder, we sway to the music for a moment before he starts to move, taking me with him. He spins me, then I'm snug to his body, and I follow his lead.

"Where did you learn to dance?"

"It was required as part of my…education."

He likes talking in code. "You're very good." He moves with such ease that it makes me feel as if I'm as good as he is, but I'm not by any means.

The music changes, and I find myself breathless against his chest. He leans in and runs his nose along my neck, inhaling my scent. "Ask me," he rasps.

I don't have to question what he means. "Kiss me," I whisper, wanting him…needing him. The anticipation of his lips on mine has my knees buckling. I want to forget about everything and be consumed by this man, if even just for one night.

His gaze flicks to mine, and I can see every movement in his jawline. My breath catches, and I inhale his masculine scent. My heart races as he sifts his fingers through my bun, and my hair falls loosely around my shoulders. His beautiful lips part, placing them on mine and dipping his tongue inside, mingling it with mine. He deepens the kiss, and my body craves him as my mind screams, *"Don't do this. You'll regret it in the morning."*

Panic sets in, and my heart ricochets. He stops kissing me and lays his forehead on mine as if he senses my hesitation. "We don't have to do this." His voice is gravelly.

His eyes are dark, yet comforting, and it settles me. "I want to," I whisper.

He tangles his hand with mine and leads me to his bedroom. Ever opens his bedside drawer and tosses a condom on the bed. He kisses me again as his hand grasps the back of my neck and then down the delicate planes of my collarbone. "You are so damn beautiful," Ever hisses against my lips. "I need you naked, now."

Judging by the erection straining against his jeans, I believe him, and it empowers me. Finding the hem of my top, I pull it over my head, thankful that I have on matching panties and bra.

"Now your pants," he orders, and I willingly follow his command, leaving me standing in white lacy lingerie.

He inhales an unsteady breath. "Damn," he chokes out.

"You like?" I rasp.

"More than anything I've seen in my entire life." He wastes no time releasing my breasts from the white lace, bending down and bringing my taut nipple into his warm mouth. I arch my back in pleasure. He teases my nipple to an almost painful point with his teeth.

My body is so sensitive to his that I feel I might burst into flames. I reach for the button on his jeans and tug at it. He nearly rips my panties off with one finger, dragging them down my thighs. As he moves me closer to his monstrous bed, he yanks his jeans and boxers off, and I stare at the size of his package.

A grin covers his face. "You like what you see?"

"Very much," I say with a nod and heat filling my cheeks.

Closing the distance between us, his large hands grasp my ass, pressing his stiff, thick cock against my stomach. "I'm not sure I can take it slow with you."

The undercurrent of his voice is so strong I throb for him to be inside me. "Don't then," I gulp.

He pushes my back to the soft mattress and climbs over me. His whiskers prick my sensitive skin as he skims his mouth south, spreading my legs with firm fingers until he has them where he wants them.

I suck in a deep breath when his tongue dips inside me, and he applies pressure to my clit with his thumb. It's been so long since I've been touched that there's no slow climb. I'm already feeling my climax. I bite my lip hard to stave it off. He continues to lap and suck my clit, and I ache.

"Don't you dare come," he warns, lifting his emerald eyes to mine. "Not until I tell you."

"I don't think that's possible," I pant.

He climbs face to face with me. "Breathe, Noa."

I inhale as he hovers over me, not moving. "Okay," I finally rasp.

He gets to his knees and grabs the condom.

"Wait," I say, rising to my elbows. "I want to touch you."

He tosses the ripped foil packet on the bed.

I cup his balls with one hand and stroke him a few times with the other and adjust my position to place his tip in my mouth.

He breathes in sharply. His chest rises and falls

quickly, but he doesn't stop me. I suck him into my mouth as far as I can, and he tangles his fingers in my long strands of hair. "Yes," he hisses. "That feels so damn good."

I lick him from my lips and draw his cock into my mouth again. When he can't take any more, he jerks free and snatches the condom, and rolls it down his length.

In this moment, nothing else exists for me. No past, no dead husband, just Ever. Unimaginable pleasure rocks me to the core when he slowly inches inside me, sizzling my skin. I can't stop my body's reaction to him, clamping down around him.

He leans down, clasping my hands above my head. "Breathe, baby, breathe." His hips find a delicious rhythm, thrusting hard, and I squeeze my eyes shut, feeling every color of my pending orgasm. It's bright orange with flames that just might burn me from the inside out.

He adjusts his hips and hits a magic spot. Then I feel his finger at my backside, applying pressure to my forbidden entrance. "Ever," I squawk his name.

"Relax and trust me."

I focus on the pleasure it brings rather than the slow, burning sensation on his entry. My body gives in to him. With his other hand, he snags my hip and pushes his cock deeper than I ever imagined it could go. My ass is on fire, and my channel is throbbing for release.

"I need to come," I gasp.

"Not yet," he grunts.

Time ticks by as I grip the sheets, feeling him so deep inside. It's pleasure like I've never felt before. My mouth falls open with a cry when he pulls out and drives back inside of me. I can barely breathe, the sensation of him filling me. I seize around him no longer in control. A jagged scream erupts from my lips.

"Shit! Noa, shit!" Ever flinches inside me and arches his back, releasing a long, sensual moan. When his body relaxes, he drops over me, sucking my tender, blush-colored nipple into his mouth.

I stare at the ceiling, not with regret but the feeling of being on the brink of satisfaction.

"We're not done. Far from it." His words tickle my skin. He gets up, and I admire his muscular ass as he strides into the bathroom and then comes back out, grabbing another condom on his way back to bed. "This time, you'll wait until I tell you to come."

"Practice makes perfect." I smirk.

After our second go-around, I'm completely

spent and exhausted, falling asleep with my back to his chest with no doubts that I'm satiated.

I awaken covered in sweat from Ever's body heat surrounding me. I lift my head off the pillow to look at the time on the clock I recalled seeing on his dresser. It's three in the morning.

My mind starts racing at what I've done, and panic rushes over me. I ease out of his arms so as not to wake him and find my clothes on the floor, thanks to the dim light coming out of the bathroom. Glancing over my shoulder, Ever is naked, lying on his stomach with a hand tucked under his pillow. My gut lurches into my throat when I see scars on his back like someone had beaten him. *Who hurt you?* My fingers linger over him, wanting to touch him, to take his pain away. "Goodbye," I whisper and tiptoe to the living room. "I need to get out of here." I fumble for my phone, and the first number that comes up is Luca's since Ever entered it earlier. I quickly dress and step out of the room, and call Luca, feeling awful when he answers in a groggy voice.

"I'm so sorry. I'll call for a cab."

"Noa," he says.

"Yeah, I wasn't thinking about the time."

"Where are you?"

"Still at Ever's."

"I live in one of the rooms downstairs. I'll meet you in the lobby."

"Are you sure? I can call a cab."

"I was instructed to be at your beck and call, and you don't want to get me fired, do you?"

"No. I'll see you downstairs."

I wait for the elevator, and I'm glad the lobby is empty other than the woman behind the counter. I look a mess, doing the walk of shame in this expensive hotel. She probably thinks me a call girl.

"Where am I taking you?" Luca asks when he sees me.

"To my sister's place."

He hands me his phone. "Plug in her address." I type the address as we walk out of the building and into the parking garage. He opens the door for me to join him in the front seat.

Throwing it into reverse, he backs out of the space, and we spiral from the garage onto the empty street.

"Does Mr. Christianson know you are leaving?" He cuts his gaze toward me.

"No…and please don't call him."

"That's not my place, ma'am."

"Thank you. How long have you worked for him?"

"Since he turned eighteen."

"So you know him very well."

"Yes."

"I'm sure you've taken many women home for him."

"Yes, but not by their own choice."

"Tell me something."

"If I can, and it's not something that betrays him."

"Is he a good man?"

"Mr. Christianson hasn't had an easy life. Tragic, really, but for the hell he's endured, I'd say yes, he's a good man."

"He told me about his mother dying when he was ten. Who hurt him so badly?"

"That's not for me to say, ma'am. If he wants you to know, he'll tell you, but I wouldn't hold my breath. He never speaks of it."

"He told you."

He sighs. "He went out and got drunk after a particularly bad night. I found him and took him home. He opened up to me in his inebriation. I'm not sure if he even remembers telling me because we've never spoken of it since."

"How sad to not have anyone to talk to. He said his mom raised him alone. Where is his father?"

He presses his lips together and doesn't respond.

"Not for you to say," I repeat his words from earlier.

I don't bother him for the rest of the ride, but profusely thank him for taking me to my sister's place.

Unlocking the door, I find Sofia on the couch. "I've been so worried about you."

"I'm sorry. I should've called."

"Did you go home with the man you were having dinner with?"

"Yes."

"Bruno says he warned you that he's not someone you should be making friends with. He said he has some sort of dangerous energy that surrounds him."

"I heard what he said, but I'm more than capable of making up my own mind. Besides, he doesn't have to worry. I won't be seeing him again." If I were sticking around, he'd be dangerous to my heart, but I don't admit that out loud.

"Did he hurt you?" She rushes over to me.

"No. He awakened a part of me I thought was dead, and I'm grateful, but we agreed ahead of time that it was only a passing thing because I have every intention of returning to Essex."

"I'm glad you're okay."

"I'm going to bed. We'll chat in the morning after I contact Kip."

I collapse on my bed, smelling Ever's lingering scent on my skin. Curling on my side, I smile and drift off to sleep.

7 EVER

Stretching and reaching for Noa, I find the spot next to me empty. "Noa," I call her name and sit on the edge of the bed, only to be utterly disappointed that her clothes are no longer on the floor where I stripped them from her sweet body. Sleep usually evades me, but I dozed so soundly I didn't hear or feel her leave my arms that I recall being firmly locked around her body once I knew she could take no more of me. Her body will have an aching reminder of where I've been, and I've never been more sexually satisfied in all my life.

Snatching my phone from its charger to call her, I realize I never got Noa's number. "It's just as well. We agreed to no strings." I stand and walk naked into my shower. Never has a woman voluntarily left my bed in the middle of the night. "She's different," I whisper. I feel something for her that has thwarted me all these years, a longing for more. I'm not immune to her like all the others, and for the life of me, I don't know why. There are so many more delicious things I want to do to her body before I can get Noa Sutton out of my system.

The cool water drips down my chest and stomach but does nothing to alleviate my erection. Firmly stroking my cock, I come easily, growling Noa's name and wishing it was her hand stroking me rather than mine. Rage fills me that I want this woman so badly, and she left my bed.

Turning off the water, I snag a towel and quickly dry off. I wrap the towel low around my waist and return to my phone I tossed on the bed.

"Luca," I say when he answers. "Did you take Noa home in the middle of the night?"

"Yes, sir. You told me if she needed anything, I was to provide it for her."

"You should've called me," I grumble.

"If I had, she wouldn't trust me again, sir."

I grind my teeth, knowing he's right. "Where did you take her?"

"To her sister's apartment."

"Text me her address and Noa's phone number," I demand and hang up.

As I get dressed, there's a pounding on my door. The doorman typically buzzes me when I have a guest arriving. That leads me to believe it's one of my family members. Sure enough, I peek through the hole and see my father's snarling face. My agitation with Noa subsides, and I'm grateful she pulled her disappearing act in the middle of the night. I don't want her involved with my family in any way, shape, or form.

"What the hell do you want?" I swing open the door, and my father barrels past me.

"Your ass back at work," he snaps, walking further into my penthouse.

"I told you, I quit." I slam the door so hard the windows rattle.

"You are so damn stubborn, just like your mother!" He opens my fridge and takes out a bottle of water.

"While we are on the subject of my mother, you know, all those years ago, I never believed she drowned in the pool. She was an excellent swimmer."

"Get to the point so you can get back to work," he huffs, twisting off the white cap.

"Did you have her killed?"

"Why would I do that?" He laughs.

"You tell me. She left you, took your son, and kept me hidden."

"She was lucky she got away with it for ten years," he grunts.

I ball my hands at my sides. "You did kill her!"

"I didn't admit to anything. Your mother, as beautiful as she was, was a foolish woman. I adored her and would've given her the world if she had asked for it." He sets the bottle on the counter and lays the palms of his hands on the breakfast bar, glaring at me.

"If that were the case, why did she leave you?"

"Because she found out what the Leone name truly meant, and it frightened her just like it should you."

"She saw something she shouldn't have, didn't she?"

"I warned her never to come to my office unannounced. She ran. I didn't find out until after she left that she was pregnant with you. My housekeeper found her pregnancy test in the garbage."

"She couldn't have been too foolish if you couldn't find her."

"I never said she wasn't intelligent, but her

actions against her own husband were brainless, knowing what I was capable of doing. She left me a handwritten note threatening to go to the authorities if I tried to find her. No one threatens a Leone." He stands tall, looping his thumbs in his belt.

Bile rises in my throat. He killed her or had her killed, but he'll never admit it. "She was smart to leave you and give me her last name."

"Enough of this shit! I need you down at the docks."

I stride to the door and hold it open. "I no longer work for you."

"You do, and you will, or you'll pay the consequences." He loses his temper, yelling as spit flies from his mouth. "I'll find your weakness and break you." He lodges a crooked finger in my chest.

"I don't have any weaknesses. You beat them all out of me when I was a kid." I gnash my teeth, wanting to choke the life out of him. "My life would've been better off as an orphan than being forced to live with you."

"You are nothing without this family, and your mother did you a great disservice keeping you from me. If you'd have grown up in my home, you wouldn't be disrespectful and soft."

"More like my brother," I scoff. "Yeah, he's a real winner, alright."

He balls his hand and raises his arm to strike me, but I clutch it in my hand before he can hit me. "You'll never lay a hand on me again, old man," I seethe.

"Someone needs to beat some sense into you," he spats.

"Get out of here and don't come back or send any of your goons!" I shove him out the door and slam it.

My head falls back, and I attempt calming breaths, but it doesn't ease my anger one bit. I want him to pay for my mother's death, and knowing my father, he writes down everything he's ever ordered and keeps it locked away in his safe. I'm itching to get my hands on it.

I'm not naive enough to think he'll just let me saunter away into the sunset without repercussions for deserting the Leone name. The last time I tried, when I turned twenty-one, he had one of his men beat me with a whip. I carry the scars to prove it, and I'm not talking about the scars on my back that were added to the ones my father had already branded me with for not changing my last name. I also knew there'd come a day I'd try again. I'm just sorry it's taken me this long. My father's sins will always be on my shoulders, but my own will dwell deep in my soul.

"I need to get the hell out of here." I call the manager of the hotel and advise him that I'll need luggage carried down in thirty minutes, then I get a hold of Luca. "Call the captain and tell him I want my yacht ready and staff on board today."

"We're going to Chelsea Piers Marina?"

"Yes. My suitcase will be downstairs in thirty minutes." I disconnect.

Several years ago, I purchased a yacht that my family knows nothing about. It's been my escape from the world, and it will be the way I finally leave Manhattan, family, and my past in the wind.

8 NOA

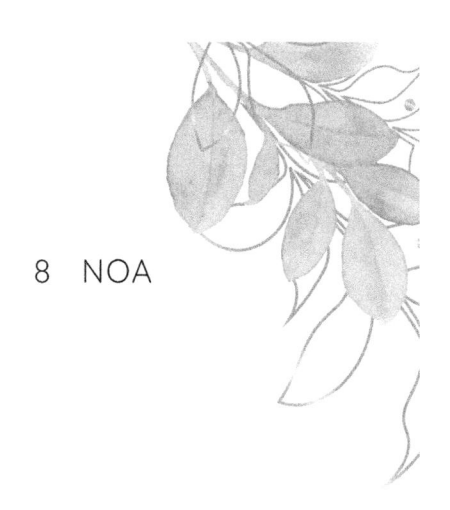

I wince, my body aching where Ever has been. When I was taking my shower this morning, I noticed fingertip bruises on my hips. Sex with Drake was good, but he was always so gentle, even when I begged him to be rough. He was afraid he would hurt me, and I wanted more. I thought our sex life was great whenever I was home, but it must not have been enough for him, or he wouldn't have turned to another woman. "Who is she?" It had to be someone he was close to. He wouldn't have had sex with just anyone.

My heart pounds rapidly with my mind running. "Sofia?" I gasp. It couldn't be. The two of them were like peas in a pod, very like-minded, and they adored each other.

I grab my purse and march into the kitchen to find my sister sipping an espresso. "I'm surprised you're still here," I say with a snip in my tone.

"I thought I'd go with you to talk to Kip this morning. You mentioned it last night in the wee hours of the morning."

"I'm capable of handling it myself," I snap.

"What's got your panties in a wad? I'd think after getting laid last night, you'd be in a good mood."

A loud exhale leaves my chest. "I have to ask you something, and I need you to be brutally honest with me."

"You're scaring me a bit." She frowns.

"I showed you Drake's notebook."

"Yes."

"I don't believe my husband would've slept with someone he didn't already know."

Her stare penetrates mine. "And you think I had an affair with Drake?"

"I'm asking you if you did."

She hops out of her seat. "I would never betray you like that, and I'm pissed that you think such a horrible thing. Drake and I were friends, yes, but he was your husband!"

I feel like a heel for even considering the idea.

"I'm sorry. I just…the fact that he cheated on me is eating me alive."

"Is that why you had sex with a stranger? You wanted to pay him back? Drake is dead. He doesn't care who you sleep with!"

"I know he's dead!" I cry. "His cheating is partially why I did what I did last night. I'm so sorry I thought it was you."

She anchors her hands on my shoulder. "I'm not happy about it, but it's understandable that you might think it was me. I loved Drake as a brother-in-law, a friend, and a boss, but it was never sexual."

"I believe you." I fold her into my arms.

"Are you okay?"

"I insult you, and you ask me if I'm alright?" I sniff.

"You've never been the type to have a one-night stand."

"It was very uncharacteristic for me, but it was amazing, and I don't regret it."

"If it will help you to move on, I'm happy for you. Are you thinking about seeing him again?"

"I'm going to handle things here and go back home. I have decided to sell the restaurant even if you don't end up purchasing it. If you're sincerely interested in buying it, I'm sure we can work out a deal."

"I've given it more thought, and I know it's worth way more than I have to offer. After all the work Drake put into this place, you deserve to get full value for it, and that's not something I will qualify for with the bank."

I step away and dry my tears. "Look over your finances and talk to whoever your finance person is and make me an offer." I sling my purse over my shoulder. "I'm going to go see what kind of negotiating skills Kip has. I'll see you at the restaurant later." I take the stairs rather than the elevator and hail a cab to Kip's firm.

The secretary waves me in when she sees me. Kip takes off his reading glasses and lays them on his desk. "Good morning," he greets me.

"I hope you were able to work out a deal."

He swallows and leans back in his chair. "I'm afraid not. They aren't willing to budge."

"There has to be something we can do. The money isn't due for another five years."

"The fine print says they have every right to call it in whenever they choose."

"Why now?"

"The value of the land has grown exponentially,

and they are counting on the loan being in default. They did offer to buy it, but it's substantially below what the property is worth. It would, however, pay off the loan."

I stand. "I'm going to go to them directly face to face."

"I wouldn't advise it." He gets to his feet.

"This coming from the man who initiated a loan with a mobster," I spat in desperation.

"I'll approach them again in a couple of days."

"We're running out of time. Damn you for putting me in this position!"

"I'm sorry."

I step up close to him. "Did you know?"

"Did I know, what?"

"That Drake had an affair?"

I get his answer when he casts his gaze downward.

"Who was she?"

He mashes his lips together.

"Tell me, damn it!"

"It ended a year before he died. How the hell did you find out?"

"I found his notebook mentioning his affair and that he needed to tell me his secret."

He hangs his head. "So you know about his son."

My eyes feel hazy, and my head spins. I falter, and Kip catches me by the waist before I hit the ground.

"Shit!" he barks.

"He has a son?" I rasp, rubbing my forehead.

"I'm so sorry, Noa. I thought you knew by the way you were talking." He walks me over to the couch and gently eases me to the cushion.

"Drake had a son, and he never thought to tell his wife!"

"He wanted to, but he said he didn't know how he'd look you in the face and break your heart. He truly loved you."

"His actions spoke louder than his words. A man that honestly loves his wife doesn't cheat on her and then keep a child a secret! And you knew this entire time!" I get to my feet and smack him in the chest.

"It wasn't my place to tell you."

"Who the hell is she!"

"Gia's sister. She has no idea her nephew is Drake's son. They hid it from everyone. She thinks it was some random guy that Angelica hooked up with one night."

"Oh my God, the lies." I feel faint again. He grabs me, and I slap him away. "Don't touch me! All I want from you is the location of the man I need to speak with about the loan."

He reluctantly writes it on a piece of paper. "If you insist on going, please let me go with you."

"No! Our friendship is over as far as I'm concerned!" I snatch it out of his hand and stomp out of his office.

"Noa!" he calls my name, but I never turn to look at him.

I walk the streets of Manhattan in a fog, not wanting to believe what I've just learned. "How could he?" Everything I thought I knew wasn't real. Drake, the one person I trusted most in this world, has ripped my life to shreds. In a matter of a few days, my life has unraveled.

When a horn blows, I come out of my daze in the middle of the busy street. "Sorry." I hold out my hands and weave between the cars to get to the sidewalk. A wave of nausea hits me, and I lean over, emptying the contents of what's in my stomach.

People sneer at me as they walk by, and one person says, "That's so gross. She was probably out all night drinking."

Wiping my mouth with the back of my hand, I toss my hair over my shoulder and search for a street sign to see where I am. I've wandered miles away from the restaurant. Waving, I try to hail a taxi, but no one stops. The subway will be swamped this time of day, and I don't think I can handle the smells without vomiting on someone's shoes.

"Luca," I utter, digging my phone from my purse.

"Ms. Sutton," he answers politely.

"I'm sorry to bother you again, but I could really use your help."

"Tell me where you are."

I give him my location.

"I'm ten minutes away. Stay put."

I pace the street corner, gnawing on an innocent nail. I need to try to handle the loan situation, but I'm raw on the inside, and I'm not sure I can cope with any more stress today. *He has a son.* Was he taking care of him? Sending her money?

A horn honks, and I see Luca pulling up to the curb. I hop in the front seat, and I'm sure I look a mess.

"Are you okay? Did someone hurt you?" He touches my hand.

Someone did hurt me, but not in the way that he thinks. "I'm alright, just received a bit of news that isn't sitting well with me."

"Do you want to talk about it? Perhaps another

set of ears would help with whatever it is?" he asks, maneuvering into traffic.

"That's sweet, but no. I'll deal with it."

"My boss was upset that you left without a word this morning."

"Really? I thought that's how he liked things."

"You're different."

I let that sink in.

"I've never seen him upset over a woman before."

I don't know how to respond. I don't regret our time together, and if I'm honest with myself, I'd like to see him again. Yet, I don't see the point other than amazing sex. My life will never be in New York again, and there's still the fact that Bruno has his reservations about him. I wonder what he would think about his sister-in-law's secret? Do I tell him?

"Ms. Sutton." Luca shouting gets my attention. "I've called your name three times. Are you sure you're alright?"

"I'm sorry. I was drowning in my own thoughts."

"Where am I taking you?"

"To the restaurant, please."

I feel his gaze cut to me every now and then as he drives, but he doesn't ask me any more questions, and I don't offer anything. He pulls up directly in front of The Italian Oven. I unbuckle and open the door.

"Thank you so much for coming to my rescue. I'll not bother you again."

"It was no bother at all, and if you need me, I want you to call me. It would make Ever happy to know that someone is looking out for you."

I lean over and kiss him on the cheek. "Thanks, Luca. You're a good man."

Slinging my bag over my shoulder, I hop out and march into the restaurant and into Sofia's office.

"Hey, how did it go?" she asks, getting to her feet from behind her desk.

"Kip wasn't able to get them to budge. They want all the money upfront or for me to sell them the restaurant at much less than what it's worth." I burst into tears.

"Oh, sweetie." She folds her arms around me. "We'll figure something out."

"It's not that," I wail and plop on her couch.

"Then why are you crying?" She gets on her knees in front of me.

"Drake has a son," I sob louder. "Please tell me you didn't know."

"What?" she gasps. "That can't be true. Where did you hear such a thing?"

"Kip told me." My body trembles uncontrollably.

"He knew, and he didn't tell you? How could Drake keep such a secret from everyone?" She sits next to me, rocking me in her arms.

"He has a son," I repeat between gulps of air.

"Where is he?"

Rage replaces my weeping. "He had an affair with Gia's sister."

"Angelica?" She wrenches her head to look at me.

"Yes!" I seethe, and she stands.

"She interned here for her culinary school. I set it up for her to work with Drake. I never saw anything between them that made me suspicious." She stops her pacing. "Except…" Her jaw grows tight.

"Except what?" I'm on my feet.

"One night, I had forgotten my phone in the office. The restaurant had already closed, and I came through the back door. Drake's car was still here, but it wasn't unusual for him to work late. I grabbed my phone from the desk, and I heard voices coming out of the kitchen. Drake and Angelica were in some heated discussion. I asked them what was going on, and they stared at each other for a moment. Drake's facial expression was odd, as if his hand had been caught in the proverbial cookie jar. He made his way over to where I was standing and put his hand on my shoulder, guiding me out of the kitchen. He told me he was lecturing Angelica on keeping such late hours and that she was going to burn herself out. Of course, I told him that was the pot calling the kettle black. Drake worked eighty hours a week." She waves off her words. "But he made it all make perfectly good sense in trying to get her to not be like him." Her brow furrows. "What was odd about it was when I came back in the morning, Drake's car was parked in the same place, but he wasn't here." She points to the ground. "Totally out of character for him, he showed up right when we unlocked the doors for the lunch crowd. We were so busy, I never asked him where he had been, and frankly, it wasn't any of my business."

"How long ago was this?"

She taps a finger to her lip. "I want to say a year or so before he died."

"That's about the time he ended things with her, according to Kip."

She covers her mouth, holding back a gasp. "Angelica has brought the boy to the restaurant to have lunch with Gia and Bruno."

"They have no idea he's Drake's son, by what Kip told me."

"I remember cooing all over him. He was three

months old and adorable. Drake sat at the table with them, and he even held him."

I sit, and my head falls to the back of the couch. "What am I going to do?"

"What do you want to do?" She sits beside me and rubs my thigh.

My head snaps up. "Was he paying her child support? There has to be some record of it."

We both get up, and I sit at her desk and log onto the computer to access the bank records for the restaurant. "He wasn't paying her out of our personal account. I would've seen it." My fingers fly over the keyboard and put in the timeframe I'm searching for in the account.

Both of us are glued to the screen, scrutinizing every payment and withdrawal.

"What's this?" I touch the screen.

"ASMS," she reads. "Reoccurring payment. Drake told me it was an LLC corporation he was supporting to help get them started. I never stopped it because it was something he wanted to do."

"Isn't Angelica's last name Scaro?"

"Yes. AS, Angelica Scaro."

"What's her son's name?"

She twists her neck to look me in the eye. "Milo."

"ASMS is their combined initials." I tap on the

link. "He's been paying her fifteen hundred dollars a month."

"I'll stop the payment." She takes the keyboard.

"No, don't. It's his son. He'd want him taken care of."

"I can't believe this has been right in front of me all this time, and I didn't see it. If Drake were alive, I'd kick his ass."

"You'd have to stand in line. I'm angry and hurt by him, but it's not the boy's fault. He deserves a good life, and I'll make sure he has it."

"What are you going to do?"

"First thing is, I'm going to confront Angelica. Then, I'm going to give her the life insurance policy on Drake that I never spent. That way, if I lose or sell this place, she'll still have what she needs to raise him." I get up and walk to the door.

"Where are you going?"

"I need a drink."

"You might want to wash your face first, or every person out there will know you've been crying."

"Good idea." I reverse my steps and use the bathroom in her office.

9 EVER

"Is that all of your luggage, sir?" Luca asks before closing the trunk.

"It will do for now." I glance at my silver watch. "I want to make a pit stop."

He gets behind the wheel, and I climb in the back seat. "A detour for Ms. Sutton?"

"Yes. Take me to her sister's apartment."

"I'd gladly do that, sir, but she's not there."

"How do you know this?" I squint.

"She was in a bit of a bind and called me. I picked her up in the middle of the city and drove her to the restaurant."

"How long ago?"

"Thirty minutes or so. I came directly here after I dropped her off."

"What was she doing wandering around in the city?"

"I don't know, but she looked a mess."

"Did someone hurt her?" I grind my teeth in an unexpected protective mode.

"No, sir. Not physically, anyway."

"Call my security team and have them observe her from a distance twenty-four seven. My father has made some threats, and if he thinks for one second that I'm involved with her, there's no telling what he will do." Luca has my trust one hundred percent, and I've always given him access to my security team.

"Are you entangled with her, sir? You seemed a bit off-kilter with Ms. Sutton leaving your place in the wee hours of the morning."

"I don't know what she is to me, but I'd like to find out and, in the meantime, keep her safe from my family."

"I like her." He smiles. "I think she'd be good for you."

"The question isn't whether she'd be good for me. It's the other way around. You know what my life is like and the constant danger I live with for being a Leone. I'd never want to bring a woman into my world."

"That's why you choose the type of women you sleep with." He nods as if he finally gets it.

"She makes me want so much more," I whisper my admission and stare out the window for the duration of the ride.

Luca finds a parallel parking space across the street from the restaurant. "I'll wait here, sir."

Dashing between oncoming traffic, I slip inside, past the people waiting in line to be seated. Bruno is at the bar and scowls when he sees me. He flings a towel over his shoulder when I wedge between two customers as he approaches me.

"I'll take a bourbon. The best you have on hand."

His jaw twitches as he reaches for the bottle and places a glass in front of me, dropping in an ice ball.

"You remembered how I like it." I chuckle.

"It's my job to recall my customer's orders."

"Is Noa in the back?"

He leans his elbows on the counter and lowers his face next to mine. "If you hurt her, I'll hunt you down. I don't give a shit about your ruthless reputation when it comes to the people I love. I might die protecting her, but make no mistake, I'll safeguard her from the likes of you."

"I'm glad to hear it. She needs someone as overly protective as you in her life, but I have no intention of harming her." I swallow the bourbon in one gulp. "I'm glad we've cleared the air between us."

"I wouldn't exactly say we've cleared the air," he grunts.

Out of the corner of my eye, I see Noa coming from the back of the restaurant. She's licking her lips and running her fingers through her hair. She looks neatly put together, but her body language tells me something is wrong. How did I get to read this woman so well, so quickly? *Perhaps it was the hours I spent getting to know every inch of her body last night.*

She does a double-take when she sees me and darts in my direction. "Hey," she says softly as a pink glow eases onto her cheeks.

"You left without a word." I flatten my lips.

"Bruno. I could use a glass of wine," she tells him. "Actually, just give me a glass and the bottle."

He hands them to her, and then she searches for an empty table and walks over to the hostess, telling her we'll be occupying it. I follow her with my gaze on her ass as she sways her hips.

I sit and wait for her to speak. "I'm sorry. I thought it would be easier than you having me escorted out of your bed."

"I had no intention of you leaving. I was looking forward to having breakfast with you."

"By that, you mean coffee," she snorts, "and watching me eat."

My head tilts to the side. "I find great pleasure in watching you eat."

Her teeth find the corner of her mouth, catching my meaning.

"I'd love nothing more than for you to be in my bed again."

"I thought we had an agreement."

"We do, but you're still in town, so why shouldn't we enjoy the time we have left together."

She sighs. "Look, my life is in an uproar, and I don't need to bring you trouble."

"Trouble is my middle name." I laugh. "I highly doubt whatever mess you're in will bring me any danger." My mess may get her killed. *So why am I sitting here with her?*

"Things are complicated." She adjusts in her seat. "You're a businessman. I could use some negotiating skills. I'm sure being a real estate mogul, you're very knowledgeable and could offer great advice."

"I'm an excellent negotiator. Shoot with your questions."

"My late husband took out a rather large loan on the restaurant a few years ago, and the money is due. This restaurant can't foot the cost of the loan. It wasn't supposed to be due for several more years, and at that time, I'm sure it wouldn't have been an issue, but the loan holder wants their money now. We offered them higher payments, but they turned it down, stating it's due in full. They lowballed an offer on the property to purchase it. What do you think the real value on this place would be?"

"Without seeing the revenue it's drawing in, I could only take a reasonable stab at the value of the property." I pull a pen from my coat pocket and write a number on a napkin and slide it across the table to her.

"Wow!" Her mouth falls open.

"If you want to list it, I can have a buyer within a week."

"I don't want to sell it to just anyone. If I'm going to practically give the place away for a steal, I want to sell it to my sister."

"Can she get her hands on a loan that large?"

"She's looking into what she can afford."

"The loan that's being called, how much is it?"

She writes it on the napkin and spins it in my direction. "I can write you a check, and we can work out new terms."

"I don't want your money." She half laughs. "Advice yes, money no."

"Alright. Offer as much cash as you can spare with an additional interest rate for the next five years. Any reasonable businessman would take you up on your offer."

"I'm not sure how sensible they are," she mutters under her breath.

"I'd be happy to make some phone calls for you if you want to give me their information."

"That's not necessary. I'll do as you suggested and counter another offer to them, but thank you for your advice."

"Whatever else that has sadness in those caramel eyes of yours is more personal." I reach over and cover my hand with hers. "You can talk to me."

"I've shared enough for one day, and me giving intimate details of my personal life would cross the line we've created." She sips her wine, leaving a light shade of pink lipstick on the rim.

"I'll take anything intimate from you I can get."

She swallows a few times and blinks. "I did rather enjoy our time together."

"Come away with me for the weekend."

"What? No, I couldn't. I have a few things I need to deal with in town."

"Whoever the loan is from won't be negotiating over the weekend, and anything else can wait."

"You make it sound so simple." She trails her finger over the rim of her glass.

"It is. Pick me." I don't let my gaze drift from hers. "Think about all the pure animalistic pleasure we can inflict on one another."

"A weekend of sex and no stress. That's pretty tempting." She scrunches her nose.

"I think you should take me up on it. I have the perfect place to steal you away. No phones, no busy streets, lots of sunshine and fresh air."

"Does a place like that exist in New York?"

"It does in my world, and all you have to do is say yes."

She drums her nails on the wooden tabletop. "I can deal with the loan on Monday, and the other, I'm dreading it anyway, so why not put it off for a few more days."

"Is that a yes?" I waggle my brows.

She grins and nods. "Yes."

"Great!" I smack the table with the palm of my hand. "I'll have Luca pick you up at six and deliver you to me."

She glances at the time on her phone. "That will give me a few hours to do some shopping."

"Make sure you buy a skimpy bathing suit. Better yet, naked still works for me." I wink, thinking how much I like this woman and how hard I am talking about her being naked.

"Don't you work?" she snorts.

"I do, but I play harder."

"I guess that's the glory of being in business for yourself, even though that never rang true for Drake. He worked upwards of eighty hours a week."

Her words ring in my ears. Now that I'm no longer employed with my father, I'll delve into a few new legit real estate projects I've been wanting to develop. "Sounds like your husband needed a vacation."

The smile she was wearing fades. "I think both of us needed to work a lot less than we did."

"Are you planning on returning to your job?"

"At some point, yes, in a different fashion. I don't want to travel anymore. I'll start a food blog. I've been compiling notes for months."

I stand. "I'll see you this evening."

As I'm walking out of the restaurant, my brother rounds the corner with an unfamiliar face. "Nick," I say, wanting to move past him.

"This is my asshole brother, Ever." He grabs my arm. "When he comes to his senses, he'll be working for our father again. This is our new associate, Victor."

He sticks out his hand, but I keep mine at my side. "I won't be returning, so the introduction is unnecessary."

Victor steps within inches of me. "He's right. You are an asshole. I'm not a Leone, but even I know you don't get to walk away."

"I didn't ask your opinion," I spat.

He shows his teeth and takes a step back.

"What are you doing at the restaurant?" My brother peers through the large windowpane.

"Whatever everyone else is doing, enjoying the food." I'd say none of his damn business, but I don't want him to suspect I'm seeing Noa.

He narrows his gaze at me. "I'd hate for our father to get wind of you working against us."

What the hell does that mean? "Strictly pleasure." I cross the road to where Luca is still waiting and climb in the back seat.

"Who's the new guy with your brother?" Luca asks, pulling into traffic.

"My father said he was hiring someone to take the load off of Nick, which means he'll be doing the dirty work."

"Nice guy, I bet." He chuckles.

"Does my father still call you?"

"Every damn day, but you don't have to worry. I don't work for him."

"Don't ever mention Noa to him, even in passing."

"I'd never disclose anything, sir."

"You're a good friend, Luca." He's way more than an employee to me. I consider him my one and only confidant.

10 NOA

When I step into Sofia's office to snag my purse, she's on the phone. I tiptoe inside and mouth the words, *I'll call you later.*

"Wait," she says, covering the phone with her hand. "I'll only be a second." She finishes her conversation with a vendor and hangs up. "When are you planning to speak with the company we owe money to. I'd really like to get it resolved before I apply for a loan."

"Monday. First thing."

"Oh." She squints. "Where are you headed?"

"I need to get out of here for a few days."

"Are you going home? You just got here a few days ago."

I debate telling her the truth, then lie. "Yes. I

promise I'll take care of things when I return, and after being at my old apartment, a couple of days has been two days too long."

"What are you going to do about Drake's son?"

"Be in denial and not think about it until Monday." I sling my bag over my shoulder.

"Are you sure you're okay?"

"I'm not, but what choice do I have. I've really got to go. I'll see you Sunday evening."

"Call me if you need to talk," she hollers as I haul tail out of her office before she asks me any more questions. I hate lying to my sister, but I'm not sure what the hell I'm even doing, and there's no possible way she'd understand. I've agreed to a weekend away with a man I've just met…and slept with. My body tingles at the possibility of being in his arms again. It's a short-term solution to my loneliness.

Bruno catches my eye and waves me over to the bar. "You really shouldn't be sharing a meal with that man. I'm telling you, he's trouble."

"You worry too much," I say and then have the strange sensation that I'm being watched. I skim the bar area, and there are two men sitting together dressed in black, and one of them is lowering his finger that was pointing at me. "Do you know those two men?" I whisper to Bruno. "One of them looks familiar."

"The one on the right was here the other day with your new friend that I've warned you about repeatedly."

That's right, it is him, but the other man isn't the same one that was at Ever's table. They swiftly shift their gazes in my direction and then away when they see me watching them.

"Do you want me to escort them out of the restaurant?" Bruno asks.

"No. I'm leaving anyway. I'll be back in a couple of days." I squeeze his arm.

Walking the streets of Manhattan, I duck into several boutiques and find a short summer dress, a pair of sandals, and a navy-colored bikini with ties holding up the bottoms. It's been years since I bought myself a new bathing suit or swam in the ocean, for that matter. The waters around Essex are cold, but I used to swim in them all the time when I was growing up. Oh, to be a kid again and not have a worry in the world.

I make it to Sofia's apartment with just enough time to pack a bag before my phone pings with Luca's number, letting me know that he's parked at the curb waiting for me.

Clutching my overnight bag, I hustle down the stairs, and I'm greeted with an open door to the front seat. "Why does Ever sit in the back?" I ask, sliding inside.

He jogs to the other side and gets behind the steering wheel. "He prefers the back seat. I think his father ingrained it in him that it was his role."

"His father. He doesn't speak of him. Is that who raised him after his mother died?"

He exhales as he bites his bottom lip. "I've said too much. Please disregard me mentioning Ever's father."

Luca keeps his secrets like a loyal friend, but it makes me that much more curious. I want Luca to trust me as much as he does Ever. "It's already forgotten," I reach over and touch his shoulder. "So, where is it that you are taking me?"

"To Chelsea Piers."

"To a marina? Is he taking me somewhere by boat?"

"I wouldn't exactly refer to it as a boat." He shrugs one shoulder.

"You've piqued my interest. I can hardly wait."

Rush hour traffic is more brutal than usual on a Friday night, and I'm antsy to get to where we are going. "These are a few of Ever's favorite songs." Luca hits a playlist on the dash.

I take in the lyrics, most of them sad, and it makes my heart ache for him. My draw to him is like nothing I've ever felt before, not even with Drake. I don't know if it's because I find him wickedly mysterious, like a forbidden fruit, or if it's his softer side he doesn't wear on his sleeve. Right now, he's a much-needed distraction from the chaos of my life. I should attach a red flag to myself to warn him to steer clear of me so I don't drag him into my baggage. I have plenty of bruises. My mind drifts to the scars on his back that I saw when he was sleeping.

"Some scars never heal," I say softly.

"Did you say something?" Luca asks, turning down the volume of the music.

"Just wondering how much longer." I squirm in my seat.

"Only a few more minutes." He looks at me as if he wants to ask me something. "I know I don't give much away about my employer…he's a good man."

"That's not what you were going to say, was it?" I twist in my seat to face him.

"He guards his heart, and I'd hate to see him give it away and be rejected."

"I don't think you have to worry about that. We're only sharing time together while I'm in New York, and I'll be going home soon."

"Still…" he says.

His heart plays on repeat in my head until we park at the marina.

"I'll grab your bag." He turns off the engine.

"No need, just tell me which boat is his."

"Walk all the way to the end of the dock and turn right. You won't be able to miss it."

"Thank you, Luca."

"Text me when you get back, and I'll pick you up."

My bag sits firmly on my hip as I make my way down the wooden dock, admiring all the boats moored to it. The ships and their sails make a beautiful picture in any backdrop, even if the water is murky and uninviting. When I get to the end of the dock, I look right, and my mouth gapes. Luca was correct. A boat is an insult to the substantial yacht anchored alongside the dock.

Luca must have announced my arrival because Ever hops down and greets me. "I see you made it safely." He kisses me on the cheek.

"Wow! This is yours?" I know he exudes an air of wealth, but this is uber-rich.

"Welcome to the Ella." He splays his hand proudly in her direction.

A hint of jealousy hits me. "This Ella must have been someone very special to you."

"Ella Christianson was my mother." He elbows me. "You weren't jealous or anything?" He chuckles. "If you were, I'd be okay with that because that means you like me."

"Don't go getting all carried away," I snort. "I'm just mighty impressed. Real estate development has been good to you."

"Are you impressed by the money or the man?" He looks serious about his question.

"As far as I'm concerned, you could own that dinghy"—I point—"and I'd be thrilled. I love going out on the water."

He places his hands on my hips. "So your answer is the man."

"Absolutely." I peck his lips.

"Good to know." He boldly kisses me.

"Keep that up, and everyone living in this marina might get more than they bargained for," I tease, feeling my cheeks turn pink.

He throws his head back and laughs. "Come on, let me give you a tour."

Polished floors slap beneath my shoes as I follow

him onto the deck, and he holds open a tinted glass door with brass handles. "This is the main deck. You'll find all the comforts of home in this room. If there's anything you need, just pick up one of the phones, and my staff will assist you."

There are two oversized sofas facing the windows that are adorned with thick white curtains. An area rug with a pale-blue pattern rests beneath the square cherry coffee table, with books laid on top of it. A bar is adjacent to the living room area, stocked with bottles of liquor.

"What? No television," I say sarcastically.

"There's a theater room on the second level, so there's no need for a television." He sticks his hands in his slacks.

"I bet you've had some hellacious parties on this ship."

"You're the only person who's ever stepped foot on it other than my staff and Luca."

I'm shocked. "I feel very special, then." I tug his hand out of his pocket and lace mine with his.

He takes me around, pointing out every detail of the yacht, and then stops in front of a door. "This is my cabin."

I lick my lips with anticipation. "Do I get to see it, or are you keeping it a secret?"

"You are most definitely going to be spending a lot of time locked in here with me. Unfortunately, at this moment, I'm needed on the upper deck to get this ship into the water. Feel free to make yourself comfortable." He tilts my chin to his lips and kisses me. "We'll be served dinner in an hour, so naked is not an option. Although, I wouldn't mind sitting across the table from you, watching you devour food with no clothes on. I'd be hard the entire time, but I'd get great pleasure from it." He smacks me on the ass before he disappears up the stairwell.

I open the door to complete luxury. A large bed sets in the middle with the most invitingly soft light-gray comforter on it with silky sheets folded down. I set my bag on a wing-backed chair and take a look around. The bathroom is bigger than my entire bedroom in Essex, and it boasts a jetted tub. On the dresser is a picture framed in black wood. I pick it up for a closer look. "I bet this is his mother." It's a young boy, approximately eight years old, with one arm wrapped around the woman's waist. She looks stunningly happy and proud of the boy at her side.

"That would be Ella."

I jump at the sound of Ever's voice. "Sorry…I was…"

"Being nosy." He grins and moves further into the room.

"I kinda was." I crinkle one side of my face. "I guess I'm curious to know more about you."

He closes the distance between us and wraps his arms around my waist. "You mean other than my mad skills in bed." He waggles an eyebrow, and I can't help but giggle.

"You left out the word massively mad skills." I place my hand on his firm chest.

"I think parts of me are substantial." He drops his gaze between us and then smiles.

"You're bad," I say with a laugh, "but very true."

"I can be as bad as you want me to be." He grows firm between us. "But first, get changed for dinner. We're going to eat on the upper deck."

"Alright." I pick up my bag and go into the bathroom, shutting the door behind me. I brush out my hair and change into the new dress I bought and my sandals. When I walk back into the bedroom, Ever is sitting on the edge of the bed, speaking in a hushed tone on the phone.

He ends the call and stands. "You look beautiful."

"Thank you."

He holds out his hand, and I take it, following him up three flights of stairs. He opens the door to the top deck, which is lit up with round white hanging lights strewn over it. There's a seating area with cushioned walnut chairs and a wet bar. A single table for two sets near the railing overlooking the water. He pulls out the chair for me to sit.

"It's the perfect evening with no rain in the forecast, so I figured it would be nice to have a meal out here."

"It's perfect."

A man dressed in black slacks and a white jacket brings over a bottle of wine. "I was advised this is your favorite, ma'am." He holds out the wine for me to read the label.

"How did you know?" I ask Ever.

"I pay attention," he mutters.

He pours both of us a glass of wine. "The appetizers will be served shortly," the man says and disappears.

"How was the rest of your day?" he asks, tipping his glass to mine.

"It was good, thanks to you. I got to go shopping and forget all about my morning."

"I'm glad you agreed to spend the weekend with me."

I'm sitting here in front of this gorgeous man, dying to get my hands on him, yet I want to take my time and get to know more about him. I want to ask him questions without betraying anything Luca mentioned.

"Your mother was a beautiful woman. You have her eyes."

"I miss her very much."

"Is your father still alive?"

He fidgets in his seat. "He's not a topic I'd like to discuss."

"I'm sorry if I hit a nerve. I only wanted to get to know you better."

He runs his tongue over his teeth. "I'd like that." He exhales. "He's not a good man, and I'd rather not speak of him."

I rest back in my chair. "Alright. Tell me something about you."

"There's not much to tell. You already know what I do for a living and that my mother died when I was young."

"Did you go to college?"

"No."

"How did you become a real estate developer?" Our appetizers arrive, and they smell like a salty heaven. "Oysters."

"One of my favorites," he says, handing me a small fork. "My mother used to take me boating when it was oyster season in Florida. We'd spend hours in the water collecting them."

"That's a great memory."

"We took many trips together, and she taught me all about things in nature and how to speak Italian."

"Sembra una madre meravigliosa," I respond, telling him she sounds like a wonderful mother.

"You speak fluent Italian?"

"My father is Italian, and my mother is French."

"I knew Sofia was an Italian name, but where did Noa come from?"

"My mother is a very religious woman and loved the story of Noah in the Bible. She insisted since my father named my sister, she got to choose my name."

"Are you close to your mother?"

I slurp an oyster in my mouth and swallow it. "I see what you did there. We were talking about you, and you flipped the conversation to me."

"You're much more interesting than I am." He scarfs down an oyster.

"I highly doubt that," I snicker.

The waiter comes back and lights the candle in the middle of the table, and refills our wineglasses.

"Would you ever consider moving back to New York?"

"No," I answer quickly. "There are too many bad

memories there, and I only resided there because of Drake."

"So, once the restaurant is sold, you'll be done with New York for good?"

"Other than an occasional visit to see my sister, yes. You being from Florida, have you ever thought about going back?"

"I don't think I could bear returning without my mother there."

"Do you like New York?"

"Not especially. I do have a favorite restaurant." He winks. "They have phenomenal Italian food," he joshes.

"What's our destination for this weekend?"

"Other than my bed, we'll be out in the open water. I have Jet Skis we can play around on if you'd like. Do you enjoy fishing?"

"Believe it or not, I really do. My father used to take me out in our John boat to fish off the shore of Essex."

"Sembra un padre meraviglioso." He smirks.

"He's the best father a girl could ask for."

The grilled steaks are delivered to our table along with fresh green beans and a sweet potato.

"This looks delicious."

He talks about things he experienced with his

mother, and his eyes light up, and he openly laughs. He's charming and very sexy. I find everything about him attractive, including his mind. When he wants to be, he can be very witty, and I love our banter. I don't see the side of him that Bruno does, and if I'd let myself, I could easily fall in love with this man. Luca's words jump into my head. *He guards his heart.* We have that in common since Drake died. I never thought in a million years I'd give mine away again, but this man sitting across from me makes me yearn to feel loved again. He's nothing like Drake at all. They couldn't be more opposite.

"What are you thinking about?" His eyes darken.

"How much I'm looking forward to going back to your bedroom with you."

He stands and offers me his hand. The energy between is palpable and most certainly sexual… and something more.

11 EVER

"You and I've burned together fast." I don't know if I'm capable of putting out the flame that's sweltering between us.

She takes the lead down the stairs, and I saunter behind her, growing harder with every single step. My gaze follows the path of her body that I'm aching to touch. I'd have taken her out on the main deck and not cared if anyone watched, but I don't want to frighten her with the indecent things I want to do to her.

As soon as I push the bedroom door open, I spin her, crashing my mouth to hers. "I want you so badly," I hiss.

"I feel the same way." Her soft pants of breath warm my lips.

"Do you trust me, Noa?"

She pushes her shoulders back to look me in the eye. "What did you have in mind?"

I walk over to my dresser and take out three pairs of handcuffs and show them to her.

"Are those for me or you?" I can feel the heat coming off her skin.

"For you, with a promise of toe-curling sex." I know she has a bad girl inside her, and I want to be the man that brings it out of her. I dangle one from my finger. "Well? What's your answer, Noa?"

She grabs the hem of her dress and pulls it off, leaving her bare, other than a thin pair of deep blue silky panties. "I trust you." She holds her wrists between us.

"Not in the front," I rasp. I see her excitement when she inhales, and her caramel eyes turn a chocolate color.

She turns and gives me her backside with her wrists waiting for me.

I softly bite the bridge of her shoulder. "I'm betting you're already wet for me." I slide my hand down her abdomen, in between her legs, and she hums when I make contact with her sweet spot. "I was right." I take the same hand and drag it across her body and put my finger in my mouth. "You taste damn good."

"Are you going to tease me or screw my brains out?"

I chuckle low in my throat and clasp the cuffs around her delicate wrists. "A little tease, a lot of fucking." I squat and run my finger along the line of her panties. "These have to go," I moan and twist my finger in the string and ease them down her legs, and she steps out of them.

"What are you going to do with the other pair of cuffs?" Her voice is heavy with lust.

"Lay belly down on the bed," I command.

"But I…"

"You said you trusted me," I remind her with a stern glare.

I yank the comforter and the sheets off, and she settles in the middle of the bed, face down. "Spread your legs."

She does without further question.

I glide my hand down her thigh to her ankle and snap a cuff on. "Beautiful," I mutter. Then I repeat the process with the other leg and clasp the cuffs to the wooden bed frame. Something in my heart twists seeing her lying there, submitting to me.

I strip out of my clothes and grab a foil pack on the bed, but I don't roll it on yet. Then I start by lying beside her, looking into her eyes. "If I do something you don't like, all you have to do is tell me to stop."

Her mouth parts, and she licks her lips. "No safe word?"

"No. Just talk to me." Straddling her, I fist her hair in my hand and kiss the nape of her neck, and lick my way down her spine. My thighs are at her knees, and I palm her butt cheeks, caressing them. Climbing off the end of the bed, I grab her hips and draw her to her knees, legs wide apart, and press my cock against her backside. "Do you feel how badly I want you?"

"Yes," she pants.

"Tell me what you're feeling, baby."

"Your passion in every touch singes my skin."

"Good. Stay exactly where you are," I command. Coming from behind her, I kneel on the bed facing her so I can have access to her gorgeous breasts. Her nipples are pointed, waiting for me. I kiss her mouth softly at first, then deepen the kiss until she's breathless. Trailing my lips down her lean neck, over her collarbone, to her taut nipple, sucking it into my mouth. She moans, and her head falls back. I dip my cock into her folds and slide in her warmth a few times.

"Please, I want to touch you," she cries.

"Not until I'm done with you." I lie flat on my back and lick my way into her folds. She whimpers loudly and tries to bring her legs together, but she can't, and I know it will prevent her from staving off her orgasm. My tongue dances in her channel, and she continues to squirm and make nonverbal noises. I don't let up until she gives in to my tongue lashing and comes in my mouth.

"Ever," she squeaks in pleasure.

I move from underneath her, then off the bed to get behind her again and position her so that I can kneel behind her. Her head falls forward, along with dark strands of hair covering her breast. My fingers fall to her ass and touch her. "Have you ever been taken here?"

She shakes her head, and I see goose bumps form on her skin.

I place my hand in the center of her back and push her forward onto her chest with her legs still wide, smearing her wetness from her folds to her backside. I nudge the tip of my cock at her entrance and ease in an inch, and she arches her back, hissing.

"Do you want me to stop?"

She shakes her head.

Slowly, I enter further, and she clamps down. "I know it burns, but try to relax and let me in."

Her chest heaves as she inhales and exhales. "Okay, I'm ready."

When I feel her relax, I reach around to the front of her, stroking her nub as I seat myself fully inside of her.

"Oh, god!" Her body convulses.

"Am I hurting you?"

"Only in a good way." Her voice sounds hoarse with need.

I knot my fingers in her hair. "Your orgasm is going to be one of the most intense you've ever felt. "Just let go. I've got you." Rocking my hips, I thrust in just to the point where I'm almost out of her, then drive deeper inside. Her moans turn into cries of ecstasy as her body writhes uncontrollably, driving her hips back. The hair around her face is damp, and she's gasping for air, riding out a powerful release.

When she's done, I pull out, roll on the condom and unlock the cuffs on her wrists. She presses up to wide knees, and the palms of her hands hold her in the middle of the bed.

"Please," she whimpers.

I sit with my legs folded beneath me between her legs, then lower her down on my cock, filling her completely. I wrap my arms around her, bracing her for the rough movements to come. "Hold on, baby." My teeth dig into her shoulder, and she hisses again. I lift my hips driving in and out, and she bounces on my lap, taking everything I'm giving her.

"Yes! Don't let go of me, and whatever you do, please don't stop." I thrust harder and faster, making her quake with another release. My growl echoes off the walls of the yacht as my muscles tense, and I bury myself inside her deeper than I thought possible. Our breathing becomes one as we detonate together. She goes to her belly, and I lay my chest on her back, sustaining my weight with my elbows. I trail my tongue along her spine. "Did I hurt you?"

"Not at all." She's still coming down from her sexual high.

I get to my knees and release the cuffs around her ankles and massage her legs. "You're going to have marks on your gorgeous body."

She swings over to face me. "I enjoyed receiving every single one of them."

I roll the condom off and toss it on the cabin floor.

"You do have more of those, right?" She braces herself on her elbows and chews on her bottom lip.

"You're insatiable." I lean over her to grab another one, but she stops me.

"Not yet." She licks her lips, and I'm lost in her.

"IT'S AFTER MIDNIGHT," I whisper next to her ear. "Are you hungry?"

"You fed me dinner, but I'm starving. You've wrecked me, and I don't think I'm capable of walking." She rolls to face me, pressing a soft kiss on my lips.

"You have no idea of the wreckage you've caused me." My heart is in shreds thinking she'll return home, and I won't see her again. "I'll have my staff bring us a plate of desserts for you to choose from."

"No, no, it's okay." She sits and winces. "I'd like to get some fresh air."

"I could always carry you in my arms."

"That would be a bit overdramatic." She laughs and flinches. "On second thought…" She smiles at me over her shoulder.

"With that mischievous smile of yours, if you

don't get your delectable ass out of bed, I'll cuff you again."

She clambers to her feet and tosses her dress over her shoulders, then blows a strand of hair from her eyes. "This will have to do."

I begrudgingly crawl out of bed. My only motivator is that I'm hungry for food. While I tug on a pair of jeans, I call my waitstaff, waking them up to prepare a tray.

"I feel terrible. We could have just raided the fridge ourselves." She stares at my bare chest.

"They are highly paid to be at my beck and call."

"Are you going to put a shirt on?" She swipes her tongue over her bottom lip.

"If your hair can be that much of a mess, then there shouldn't be an issue with me not wearing a shirt." I chuckle.

She runs over to the mirror, leans her head to the side, and brushes it with her fingers. I walk up behind her and slap her in the ass. "I'm still not wearing a shirt." I take her hand and walk out of the cabin to the upper deck, where one of my employees is turning on the gas firepit and has already brought out a bottle of wine.

"I'm parched. I could really use a glass of water." Noa snuggles into my side as if she belongs there.

"Bring two glasses of water with our dessert," I tell him. The chair scrapes the wooden deck when I pull hers next to mine, not wanting to have any distance between us.

"May I ask you something?" She sits.

"After the trust you just showed me, you can ask me anything."

"Why are you so guarded with your past?"

"I said you could ask. I didn't say I'd answer."

"Alright, let's play a game. I'll tell you something personal, and then you share with me. I'll even go first." She lays her hands in her lap, and her shoulders rise with her inhale. "I just found out my husband had an affair."

I shift in my seat and take her hand in mine. "I'm sorry."

"Your turn," she says unblinkingly.

"Wait…can't we discuss your feelings about it. I mean, it has to be difficult because you can't even confront him with what you know."

"That's probably a good thing," she scoffs.

"How did you find out?"

"I visited the place we shared, and I found a notebook in his handwriting."

"It was my fault. I should've been here with my husband, not traveling around the country…for what?"

That's what she was crying about in the apartment when I saw her. "Did he mention who it was?"

"No, but I found out from his best friend, Kip."

"Kip Oliver?"

She squints. "You know him?"

"Yeah, I've used his firm on several projects." I don't divulge that he's the architect that handles some of my family's business.

"He knew, and he didn't tell me."

"I'm not taking his side or anything, but if they were best friends, it would be bro code that he couldn't tell you."

"In the two years my husband has been dead, I think he should have informed me."

"Why? To sour your memories of the man you loved?"

Her shoulders drop with a deep exhale. "Because he fathered a child."

"Ouch." I caress her hand with my thumb.

"Needless to say, we're no longer on speaking terms."

I'm sad for her but happy that she'll steer clear of him. "I don't blame you."

"Now, tell me something about you."

I stare at her.

"How about if I ask you something specific?"

"Okay," I draw out the word.

"How did you get the scars on your back?"

"Perhaps something easier?"

"Who did you go to live with after your mother died?"

"My father."

We're interrupted by a platter filled with different types of desserts being placed in front of us.

"Don't you want to discuss it?" She throws my words back at me.

"No. I answered your question." I cut off a piece of strawberry cheesecake with my fork and hold it out for her to open her mouth.

"Just no?" She raises both eyebrows.

I nod, and she takes a bite, scraping her teeth on the fork.

"This child that your husband fathered, are you wanting to meet him?"

"The only thing I want is to make sure he's financially taken care of. He's Drake's son, and he should have his money."

"That's very big of you."

"In my mind, it's the right thing to do." She picks up her own fork and scarfs down half a piece of cheesecake, and I polish off the other half and then delve into the rich chocolate cake.

"My father," I say between bites.

"Your father what?" She stops her fork midway to her mouth.

"He left the scars."

12 NOA

No wonder he's so guarded. How could a father cause that kind of pain? "I honestly don't even know how to respond to that without being full of disdain toward your father." He lets go of my hand, and I draw it back into mine.

"Disdain is a mild word compared to what I feel for my father."

"Do you still see him?"

Way more than I'd like. "Not any longer."

"Good, because if I ever had to meet him, I'd scratch his eyes out."

He full on laughs. "I like this feisty side of you." Then he grows serious. "But I wouldn't be worth it."

I fold my finger under his chin and position him to look me in the eyes. For the first time, I see how deep-seated his pain really is. "Why would you say that?"

"Because my heart is calloused."

"I don't think that's true. All I've seen from you is kindness…maybe a beast in bed," I tease to lighten the moment.

He scoots his chair back and walks over to the rail, gripping it with both hands, looking out over the dark water.

Dabbing my mouth with my napkin, then tossing it on the table, I stand and stroll over to him, wrapping my arms around his waist from behind him.

"As much as you think you're a bad man, all you've shown me is goodness."

"Stick around, and the ugly will come out." He turns in my arms. "But I'm glad you see the good in me."

"If you look hard enough in the mirror, you'll see it too." I kiss the dimple in his chin.

"What do you say we go back to bed?" he growls.

I peek over my shoulder. "That lounge chair looks like a good place to curl up."

"I wasn't talking about sleeping."

"Neither was I." I let go of him, and as I pad over to the chair, I strip out of my dress and then curve a finger at him. "Come here."

"HAVE YOU EVER RIDDEN A SEA-DOO BEFORE?" We watch as his crew lowers one into the water.

"Yes, many times. You do have two of them right? Otherwise, you're riding bitch." I smile.

He holds up two fingers to the man lowering it to bring out another one.

I shield my eyes from the sun. "Where are we?"

"This area is called the West Hampton Dunes."

"It's beautiful."

"This is the part of New York I love."

"Then you'd like Essex. Is the beach always this secluded, or did you pay to have it private for the day?" I elbow him in the side.

"See that house on the end?"

"The big white one?"

"I own it. I purchased it a few years back, and I've never been inside."

"What?"

"One of my trips out here in the yacht, I saw a for sale sign on the property, and I picked up my phone and purchased it from right here on this deck."

"How come you bought it if you didn't plan on living in it or renting it out?"

"I don't know. Perhaps I was waiting for the right

reason to make it my own. Do you want to go explore it?"

"Absolutely, I do." I jog down to the platform where the Sea-Doos are and shred out of my cover-up.

"Unless you want me to have a hard-on the entire day, you need to put that back on. I'll gladly help you out of it once we are on the beach."

"I thought you wanted me in a barely there bikini," I snort.

"I do, but not when I can't get my hands on you." He straddles the Sea-Doo, adjusting the bulge in his crotch, and I put my cover-up back on.

"I wouldn't want you to be uncomfortable for the ride." I wink, put it back on, and turn the key over. "I'll race you," I holler, taking off over the water.

My heartbeat roars with excitement in my ears like I haven't heard in years. The wind blowing in my face, and the salty mist of the water splashing against my skin, is exhilarating, and there's a freedom to it. I make a sharp turn sending a wave of water over me, and then squeeze the handle and bolt by Ever, soaking him. He laughs and drives in a circle drenching me.

"Two can play that game." He's all smiles, and it's

good to see him having fun rather than being so serious.

We race to the beach in front of his house and dock the Sea-Doos in the sand. He spreads his fingers wide for me to take his hand. I love that he wants to touch me whenever he's near me. He's starting to feel like someone I don't want to leave.

"This is even more gorgeous up close and personal. I love the blue trim and the wraparound porch. It has an ocean view from every angle."

He digs a set of keys from his board shorts, and we stomp up the blue steps. The door hinges squeak in protest from the salty air.

"You first," he says, opening it.

The old original floors are beautiful but in dire need of stripping and polishing. A large crystal chandelier hangs in the entryway. "This feels like a home you'd see in Cape Cod." I run my hand along the white wainscot in the hallway, making my way to the kitchen with an island bar that runs the entire length of the room.

"Wow!" I spin in a circle, taking it all in.

He stands in the middle of the room with a single finger tapping his lip. "I was originally thinking I would modernize it a bit…"

"Don't you dare," I cut him off. "If anything, you should restore it to its natural beauty."

He grins. "Any other suggestions?"

I purse my lips and keep looking around. "If I made any changes to the original concept, I'd remove this wall and open up this space so the sun shines in here, and it would also give you the perfect view from this window." I walk over to it and pull back the dusty curtains.

"I like that idea. What I'd like even better is to see that bathing suit of yours now." His stride in my direction is deliberate and sexy.

"Don't you want to tour the rest of the house?"

"In due time." He fists the hem of my cover-up in his hands and yanks it off of me.

I'm breathless waiting for his next move.

He runs his finger under the strap of my triangle top and pulls it down my arm, exposing my left breast, where he proceeds to plant his mouth. "You're salty," he mumbles, teasing my nipple with his tongue.

My head falls back, soaking in the pleasure.

"I love these," he says, tugging at the strings on my hips and untying them. "Easy access."

The bulge in his board shorts is calling to me. I

undo the white string and the velcro, setting his cock free and cupping him in my hand.

"I don't have a condom," he growls.

"I thought you were a Boy Scout." I tease his lips, nipping them with my teeth.

He picks me up, and I drape my legs around his waist as he walks with his hands cradling my ass until I feel my back slam against a wall. "You're my heaven and hell." His voice is heavy. "The time I spend with you is heaven. The thought of you leaving is hell." In one slick move, he drives inside me over and over, hitting the spot he knows so well. It's not slow and easy, but rather as if he's trying to climb inside of me and claim me, and I let him.

"You feel so damn good skin to skin," he hisses.

I detonate into a frenzied orgasm so quickly.

"Shit!" he shouts and abruptly pulls out of me, grasping his dick and pumping until I feel warmth dripping on my stomach.

I wrap my arms around his head, and he buries his face between my breasts. "Sorry. I didn't mean for that to happen so fast."

"Don't apologize. I love your passion." I slide down his body and replace my bathing suit while he fixes his shorts and searches the kitchen for paper towels.

"How about we tour the second floor?"

As I wander up the stairs, I imagine the pictures that used to hang from these walls and want to know the history of the family who lived here. "Do you know the people that owned the house?"

"It was an older couple. They raised their kids here, and when the man's wife died, he said he couldn't live here with all the memories. At least that's what he told his realtor that sold me the place."

"I bet it was filled with lots of love." I poke my head into one of the bedrooms. "This was probably one of his kid's rooms. How many bedrooms are there?"

"Five."

"Do you ever want children?"

He stops walking. "I'm getting a little too old to start a family."

By the frown on his face, I don't think that's really what he was going to say. "Nonsense. You're not that old."

He continues walking down the hall to the master bedroom. "I could see us making love in this room."

"You mean now?" I point at the floor.

He peers at his crotch. "I think I need a little

more recovery time. You've been wearing it out." He glances up. "I meant in the future."

I swallow. "I thought we were keeping things casual."

"We are, but surely you'll come for a visit every now and then."

Stepping up close to him, I brush a piece of hair from his forehead. "Is that what you want? For me to come visit?"

He opens his mouth and shuts it, only to open it again. "Yes, and so much more, but I'm not in a position to offer you more."

I let my hand fall to my side with disappointment. He's gotten under my skin in a short period of time, and part of me would like to see where things could go between us, but the other part of me is still in turmoil given what I've just learned about Drake, and not ready to risk my heart. "You could come see me in Essex."

His jaw flexes with something he's not telling me. "Perhaps we could meet in the middle."

I resolve not to question him and return to exploring the house. We make our way downstairs to the deck overlooking the ocean. "I think if I owned this house, I'd never leave this spot. Imagine the sunrise, lounging in a bed swinging from this ceiling?"

"We don't have to imagine. I'll have my staff bring over pillows and blankets, and we can sleep right here tonight."

"And give up the luxury of your yacht?" I snicker.

"I'd sleep anywhere with you."

He says his heart is calloused, yet, he says the sweetest things to me. My heart aches at the thought of saying goodbye to him.

13 NOA

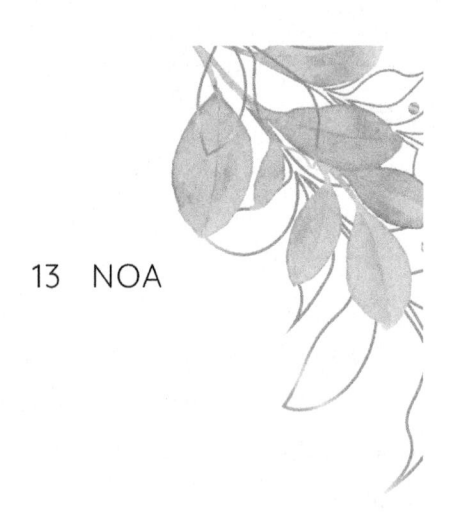

N oa

"SORRY, I didn't mean to wake you, Ms. Sutton." One of Ever's staff sets a carafe of coffee and one mug on the deck next to me.

I stretch, feeling sore from sleeping on the ground and everywhere Ever claimed me under the midnight stars. "Where is he?" I sit, looking for Ever.

"He received an urgent phone call and rode back to the yacht. He asked me to make sure you have everything you need."

"Is he coming back?"

"Yes, as soon as he's done. What would you like for breakfast? I can have it brought to shore for you."

"I'm good with coffee for now." He fills the mug, handing it to me. "How long have you worked for Ever?"

"I've been in Mr. Christianson's direct employment for a year."

"What do you mean, direct employment?"

"Up until last year, I worked for his family."

"So, you know them?" I tug the sleeping bag over my shoulders.

"Yes. Is there anything else I can get you?" He clasps his hands in front of him.

"Did you like working for his family?"

"I'm not at liberty to discuss my previous employer, but I can tell you that Mr. Christianson is nothing like them, and he treats all his employees well."

His father must really be ruthless if they are instructed not to talk about him. I mean, I've witnessed the scars he's left on Ever; it's no wonder he wants nothing to do with him. "That's good to know. Thank you. I don't need anything else."

He nods and trots across the sand to the dinghy he drove to shore. Uncovering, I get to my feet and lean against the railing, sipping my coffee and watching the sky gradually bring in the colors of the day with faint pinks and oranges on the horizon.

Last night with Ever was amazing. Never in a million years did I think when I came to New York this week that I'd be enjoying myself with a stranger or that I'd ever agree to a no strings attached relationship. He's the best thing that's happened to me in a long time. I feel renewed and not like the sad, lonely widow I'd succumbed to the past two years. He's the push I needed to open up my heart again and feel like my life isn't over. It's given me the strength I need to confidently deal with the business at hand.

After the sun has risen and Ever has still not returned, I meander into the house, envisioning what it would feel like to live here with him. Strangely, it comforts me, and that's something I'd like to hold on to, but it will never happen. We live in two different worlds, and we've both made it clear that this thing between us is only temporary, yet somehow, he's embedded in my heart.

"Get your act together, Noa," I scold myself. "This isn't reality. It's a temporary fix, and then you'll go back home." I head back outside and pour the rest of my coffee in the sand, and lay the mug on the deck. Trudging through the white sandy beach, I hop on the Sea-Doo and take it for a ride further down the island and pick up speed to ride the wake of a fisherman's boat. I lose all track of time, thrilled to be out in the salty water and the warmth of the sun kissing my skin.

I start to head back, and I see a Sea-Doo in the distance hauling ass in my direction with water shooting straight up from the tail end. I motor forward, realizing it's Ever. He comes to a quick stop next to me.

"Don't ever disappear on me like that again." His teeth gnash.

"You were tied up, and I wanted to go for a ride."

"You had me worried sick!" he snaps and runs a hand through his wet hair.

"What are you so upset about? When I woke up this morning, you weren't beside me. You left to handle a call. Did something happen?"

"I had business to take care of, and I made sure you knew where I was, unlike you who just left."

I've not seen him angry. Is this the side that Bruno was warning me about? "I'm going to head back to the yacht to get cleaned up. When you calm down, we can discuss whatever's eating you. I'm not your prisoner, and I won't be treated like one." I clutch the handle and drive past him, hitting the highest speed it will allow, only slowing down when I reach the yacht and stop alongside it for one of the crew to assist me onto the deck.

"Noa! Wait!" Ever yells my name pulling up to the landing. He hops off and runs the three steps to get to me. "You're right. I'm sorry. Please forgive my outburst."

His eyes rocking back and forth with mine are filled with sincerity, and my anger subsides. "You're forgiven, but I'm still getting a shower." I turn from him and march across the deck.

"Am I welcome to join you?" He keeps pace with me.

"I'd like to shower alone." I swing the door open and stomp down the hall to the stairs and into his cabin and directly into the bathroom and turn on the hot water. Two showerheads steam up the shower and fog the glass door. Stripping from my wet clothes, I stand in the middle letting the water soak both sides of me.

"I thought I was forgiven?" Ever is standing outside the door with his arms crossed over his bare chest.

"Fine," I mutter and slide the door open. "But I'm not in the mood to fool around."

"I'll keep my hands to myself if that's what you want."

"It's not your hands I'm worried about."

He chuckles. "May I wash your hair?" He steps in behind me.

"You know as soon as you put your hands on me, you'll be hard.'"

"I'll deal with it," he says and picks up a bottle of shampoo.

"Why were you so upset?"

"My heart started racing thinking something happened to you. It's my job to keep you safe."

"We're out here in the ocean by ourselves. What did you think could possibly happen to me?" When he doesn't respond, I turn to face him. "Talk to me, Ever."

"There are things from my past that you don't know that could put your life in danger." His jaw flexes.

"What things?"

"I'm not a saint, Noa."

"What does that mean?"

"It means your friend was right to warn you to stay away from me." He doesn't blink.

"We've all done things we're not proud of, and if it's something concerning your father, honestly, I'd look the other way." I touch one of the scars that dips over his shoulder.

"My whole life has been controlled by him, and I'm desperately trying to change that." He tucks his hand on the back of my neck underneath my soaking wet hair. "You make me want so much more than I deserve."

I take a step back. "None of this is real. You and I agreed to keep this casual."

"That's the thing. This is more real than I've ever experienced. I don't want to let go of what's growing between us."

Do I admit I feel the same way out loud? "Our worlds are so different."

"They don't have to be." He gently kisses my parted lips. "You feel the gravitational pull between us. I know you do. I can see it in the way your body reacts to my touch."

"That's just sex, Ever," I rasp against his lips, wanting to deny my growing feelings for him.

He pulls back to look me in the eye. "Is that all this really is for you?"

"I…I…no." I exhale. "But I'm not ready to go all in. I have some things I need to settle first."

"I can respect that because I do too."

"You want more from me, then you have to give

me more of you. Your secrets will destroy any chance that we have to make this work."

"I know, and I promise in due time, I'll tell you everything. You knocked the wind out of me the moment I laid eyes on you. I knew damn good and well one night with you would never be enough. In all my thirty-eight years, I've never given my heart to another human being. I want to give mine to you."

"This has all happened so fast. A couple of days ago, I was still mourning my husband, and now I'm in the middle of the ocean with a man I barely know and wanting more, but I can't give you my heart in return until it's not broken anymore."

"I'll heal it for you," he whispers with his forehead pressed to mine.

"That's a task I need to handle on my own, Ever."

He gently places his hands on my shoulders and turns my back to his front, and squeezes shampoo in his hand. "I'll wait as long as it takes."

The depth of what he feels for me is overwhelming. I believe him when he says he's never given his heart away, but I have, and I know the heartache all too well that comes with it.

He washes my hair, then my body, taking his dear sweet time, his cock straining for relief, but he doesn't make a move to take care of it. When he's done, he quickly washes himself, then turns off the water, pushes the door open, and grabs a towel. "Lean over," he instructs, and I do as he says. He lays a warm towel over the back of my head and lightly massages my scalp, drying it. "Stand up," he says, and I do. He wraps the towel snuggly around my head, and water drips down my chest. I grin when I see him lick his lips, staring at my firm nipples.

"You have such restraint," I tease.

"Believe me, I'm dying on the inside wanting to touch you, but I'm doing what you asked of me." He reaches and picks up another towel out of the warmer and softly dries down my neck, over my breasts, then my stomach, and he looks me in the eye when he's at my most intimate part, but he doesn't say a word. He travels further south, drying my thighs all the way down to my toes.

It's the most sensual thing I've ever felt, and my body is totally alive. "Hold your arms out." His voice is husky, and he's fighting for control. He sweeps the towel around me and tucks it together above my breasts. I step out, and he snags a towel for himself.

"My turn," I rasp.

"If you touch me, I'm done," he growls.

"You're a man of steel. I'm sure you can handle it."

I smile. "Turn around." I use the same commanding voice he used with me.

His jaw twitches along with another body part, but he faces the other way. Slowly, like he did with me, I dry his shoulders, his upper back, and then the curve of his back where it meets his ass. My mouth is drooling over his muscular body, and he has one fine ass. He presses his palms flat on the tile. "You're killing me," he moans, clearing his throat.

"I love that I have such an effect on you." I pop him on the backside with the towel, and he spins around. My mouth waters at the sight of his cock. "Now the front." I smirk.

"I think I'll handle it from here." He reaches for the towel, but I jerk it away.

"Nope. What's good for the goose is good for the gander."

"My gander is throbbing for your goose." His eyes narrow.

I pat the front of him dry and feel his stare all over my body. Precum is pooled on his tip, and he widens his stance when I lick my lips. "I'd be very careful not to stand too close if I were you unless you want to get dirty again."

"You don't scare me." I leer at him. Unable to control the need bounding between my thighs, I dip my head down and suck him into my mouth. He hisses and bolts his hips forward.

"Shit!" he yells and explodes on my tongue, and I drink him in. His head falls back, and he fists his hands in my hair. "Noa." He utters my name as if it's heaven to him.

I wipe my mouth with the towel and then his now-limp body part. "So much for the man of steel," I tease.

His gaze sharpens on mine. "My turn."

I squeal and run into the bedroom, where over the next hour, he gloriously devours me, and I let him.

"WE HAVE to get out of bed. I'm starving, and I want to get some sun," I mutter, crawling out of his arms. Wanting to let the daylight in, I meander to the window and open the blinds. "We're out to sea. I didn't feel the boat moving."

"That's because you were trembling in ecstasy." He laughs and slithers out of bed, putting on a pair of shorts. "I have a special treat for you today."

"You mean you planned something other than being in bed?" I tease.

"If you want to eat, you're going to have to catch your meal."

"We're going fishing."

"Even better. We're going to get our own lobster, and my staff will be on standby to throw it in a pot."

My smile grows wide. "You're right. That is way better. I've never caught my own lobster."

He ambles over to the dresser, where I threw in a few of my clothes and rummages through it. "Do you have anything you can wear that's not going to have my dick hard all day?"

"Not if I plan on getting any sun," I snort. "We might need to buy you a pair of blinders."

"Mmmm..." he hums and looks mischievous. "A blindfold."

"That's not what I said, mister." I wag a finger at him and can't help but laugh. This man, I really like as opposed to the angry one from this morning.

"Get dressed. I'm going to see how much longer it is to our destination."

"I'll meet you on the main deck." I playfully swat his ass before he walks out the door.

He glances over his shoulder. "I like this thing between us."

"Me too," I admit.

14 EVER

"I loved being lost in your arms this weekend." I nuzzle my nose in the crook of her neck. "But remind me never to compete with you again on catching lobsters. I've eaten so many I don't think I'll ever want another one."

"I won't ever be able to see one without thinking about you. Thank you so much for sweeping me away. It was exactly what I needed."

I take her hand and lead her down the dock to dry ground, where Luca is waiting for her.

"Aren't you riding with me?"

"I'm afraid not. I like helping the crew get the yacht settled." I don't want to tell her that I'm not going back to my penthouse. Her curiosity will bring questions I'm not ready to answer.

"Just as well. You'd just distract me from what I need to do."

"You're going to see the boy, aren't you?"

"Yes. The sooner I do, the sooner I can move on with my life."

"I'd offer to tag along, but I'm sure you're going to tell me it's something you want to handle on your own."

"I do, but thanks for the offer." She ducks her head to crawl into the front seat, and I snag her hand.

"When can I see you again?"

"It might be several days. Besides, you need to get back to work."

"I'll miss you in my bed."

She wraps her arms around my waist and looks me in the eye. "How did we get here?"

"I don't know, but I'm glad we are. I'll call you." After I've thoroughly kissed her one more time, I shut the door and watch Luca drive off.

Padding back to the yacht, my mind flashes to waking up next to her this morning in my bed. I woke up in the wee hours of the morning, drifting in and out of sleep and in between, making sure I was touching her. I had no desire to leave or even ever move again. She was right where I wanted her to be.

For the longest time, I watched the steady rise and fall of her chest, comforted in knowing she was safe in my arms. When I finally returned to the deck where I left her sleeping, my heart started racing with all sorts of ideas that somehow my family had gotten to her. I was frantic and lost my shit. When I found her, I was so relieved yet pissed. She didn't deserve my wrath, and I'm glad she stood her ground with me. She has guts and handles herself very well, not tolerating my crap.

When she rolled into my arms this morning, still asleep, I inexplicably wanted to kiss her. To trail my lips from the nape of her neck to her shoulders and not stop there. She'd given herself freely to me this weekend, completely trusting I was going to take care of her deep-seated desires, and I find her utterly intoxicating. My fingers idly traced her jawline, and she opened her eyes.

"You're beautiful," I said breathily.

She grinned and crawled on top of me, straddling my waist, and we made love on her terms, not mine.

"You have a phone call, sir," the deckhand hollers when he sees me. "It's important. It's the manager of the Ritz-Carlton."

I bound up the stairs, take the phone from his grip, and pace the deck. "Yes," I answer.

"I'm sorry to interrupt you, Mr. Christianson, but I wanted to inform you that there was a break-in of your penthouse."

"There are cameras everywhere. Did you see who it was?"

"Whoever did it disabled all the camera's from the fifth floor up. According to the police, whoever it was, was searching for something."

"Were there any damages to the penthouse?"

"Only minor, sir."

"Charge it to my bill. I'll be there later today to clear out the rest of my things."

"The police have requested your presence at the station, sir."

"I'll make contact with them. Thanks for calling me." I hang up. "Damn it!" I switch to Luca's number. "As soon as you drop off Noa, I'll be needing a ride to take care of some business. I know she's in the vehicle with you, but did you set up security to follow her?"

"Yes, sir. It's already begun."

"I'll need you to move out of the Ritz-Carlton. You can stay on the yacht until I can figure out something else."

"Will do, sir."

"Thanks for being discreet."

"All in a day's work, sir."

The next phone call is to my father. "What were you looking for in my apartment," I growl.

"I don't know what you're talking about," I hear a low chuckle on the other end of the line.

"Like hell you don't."

"You might as well come crawling back to your family on your knees. I told you I'd make your life miserable if you didn't. Where were you all weekend?"

"You really think I'd tell you," I scoff.

"I require your assistance on a job."

"Go to hell!"

"Check your bank account. It's empty, and until you do as your told, it will stay that way."

"I don't give a shit about the money!"

I hear his chair squeak. "I'll find what you do care about and destroy it."

"I quit giving a shit about anything years ago." *Noa.*

"Everyone has an Achilles' heel."

"Even you," I snarl.

"I took care of my soft spot a long time ago."

Bastard. He's referring to my mother. *Don't lose your cool. Get the upper hand.*

"Meet me in my office by five today, or you'll

force me to have you physically brought to me," he seethes.

I hang up, wanting to crush my phone in the palm of my hand. "I have to be smarter than him." I log onto my bank accounts, and sure enough, he drained the one I left open, but the other accounts that he has no knowledge of are all intact. If he'd agree to let me walk away, I'd give him every dime of it and start over somewhere else. Essex comes to mind with a beautiful, long-haired raven.

My phone lights up with a text from Luca letting me know he's pulling into the marina. Closing my laptop, I lock it in my safe and jog up the stairs, off the deck, and onto the dock. I rush to the vehicle and climb in the front seat, and Luca stares at me.

"What?"

"You never ride in the front seat."

"That changes today," I say, fastening my seat belt. "It was something my father insisted on and a habit I'll be breaking."

"It's about damn time." He smiles and puts the car in drive. "Why are you having me move out of the hotel?"

"The penthouse was broken into over the weekend. It appears nothing was taken, but they were searching for something."

"By they, you mean your family."

"Our family has lots of enemies, but I'd lay my life on the fact that it was a family member or one of their employees."

"Do you have any idea what they would have been looking for?"

"I keep copies of all the transactions I've made. Me walking out on them, I'm sure they are worried that I'll show them to either one of their enemies or the authorities."

"Is that where you keep the copies?"

"No, and for your protection, I'd rather not tell you the location."

"Understood, sir."

"Did you notice anything out of the ordinary when you dropped Noa off at her sister's?"

"No, and I waited until your security team parked outside of her building."

"Thanks for handling it and driving her around. I'll make sure to compensate you in your next paycheck."

"No need, sir. I rather enjoy her company."

"So do I," I whisper, and make a few phone calls to clients on the way to the Ritz.

Luca parks, and I run inside to find the manager, who is in his office speaking with a police officer.

"Perfect timing," the manager says, getting to his feet. "It will save you a trip to the police station. This is the officer going over the details of the break-in."

I shake the officer's hand. "I don't know how much help I can be. I was gone the entire weekend."

"Do you have any enemies, Mr. Christianson?"

"I'm a businessman. I'm sure I've pissed off a few people."

"You were targeted specifically."

"I understand, but nothing was taken, and I've already agreed to pay for any damages to the penthouse. If you'll excuse me, as I've said, I was gone, and I've got work to do. The penthouse will be empty by the end of the day," I tell the manager.

"If I have any further questions for you, where can you be reached?"

"The manager has my number," I say, hustling out of his office. The elevator is empty when I duck inside and ride it to the penthouse. Tables and chairs have been toppled over, and my couch is cut to shreds. "He actually thinks I'd be stupid enough to hide something in my couch?" I scoff. Bottles of bourbon lie broken on the floor, and pictures hang crooked on the wall. The clothes I left behind are in a pile on the floor, and my mattress is also sliced to shreds, lying on its side.

I grab a few articles of clothing and haul ass back to the car. "I need you to make arrangements for the rest of my things to be removed from the penthouse. Have them delivered to a storage unit. I don't want my name in connection with the marina. Have the team gather your belongings and have them delivered at the same time. And be very diligent to make sure you're not being followed. I don't want you stepping foot in the Ritz-Carlton again."

"Where to now, sir?"

"My father's office."

I take a few calming breaths before I press the phone to my ear, calling Noa.

"Hey," she answers sweetly.

"I miss you already."

"The feeling is mutual."

"What are your plans for the day?"

"There's not much of the day left. I'll spend a few hours with Sofia when she gets home and then tuck myself in early."

"I wish I could be there to tuck you in."

"I wouldn't get any sleep if you were here," she laughs.

"True, but you'd be in my arms."

"I hear Sofia's keys in the door. I'll call you tomorrow."

"Sweet dreams." I hang up, and Luca cuts his gaze to me. He's sporting a cheesy smile.

"She's good for you. Your mother would be proud."

"I have a lot of things to change in order for her to have been proud of me, but I plan on making it happen."

"If you've cut ties with your old man, why am I taking you to his office?"

"I need him to think I'm crawling back to him in order to get the proof I need that he murdered my mother."

His mouth falls open. "You think he killed her?"

"Yes, and I'm going to prove it if it's the last thing I do in this world. She didn't deserve to die at his hands."

"Let me know what I can do to help."

"My father needs to think he has the upper hand. Whatever you hear about me, play along so he doesn't get suspicious. I'm going to rent two apartments not far from his building. I'll put one in your name and one in mine. Park your vehicle there at night. Go in the front of the building, and then walk out the back. I'll have another car waiting for you in a parking garage on the corner of the block."

"What are you going to do when you find the proof you need, sir?"

"I plan on destroying him and everything he's worked to build. It will be far worse than killing him with my bare hands."

He pulls up to the building and parks. "I won't move a muscle," he says.

"Do you have the gun I gave you?"

He taps the center console.

I nod and jump out, swinging open the doors and taking the stairs to my father's office.

He glances at his watch when I walk through the door. "You had one minute to spare."

I sigh and sit. "I'm here."

"I presume with your tail between your legs. I knew money would speak to your cold heart."

His is as icy as they come. "What do you need me to do?"

"That's more like it." He unlocks a drawer and hands me a file. "There's a piece of land with a rundown warehouse on it. I want you to purchase it for me for a steal."

I look over the information. "It's on the docks. It will be very expensive."

He scribbles on a pad of paper and pushes it toward me. "This is what you'll offer."

I chuckle. "You're out of your mind. No one would accept this offer."

"You'll offer it, and he'll take it."

"Or what?"

"Or you'll threaten his twin daughters."

I close the file and toss it at him. "That's not how I operate."

"Then you'll start."

I grit my teeth and keep my mouth shut.

"Your brother and Victor are working on another piece of property that I'll be acquiring, and it's worth its weight in gold."

Poor unsuspecting person who he'll be strong-arming. "Anything else?"

"Once you've proven to me that you can handle this and that you're on board, I'll have plenty for you to do."

"Fine," I say and walk out of his office. I look over my shoulder to make sure he stays put and duck into an empty dark office, tugging my phone from my back pocket. "Luca," I keep my voice low. "I want you to drive off. I'll text you where to pick me up."

"Yes, sir," I hear him start the engine.

I don't have to wait long before I hear my father come out of his office. I peek through the slit in the blinds and watch him turn out the lights. I wait until the elevator pings and the doors close behind him.

Creeping out, I fast-pace it to his office and go to turn the doorknob, but it doesn't twist. It doesn't surprise me. He always locks his door every time he steps outside of it, even if it's just to get a cup of coffee.

I take out a credit card and place it between the lock and the doorjamb. Keeping my hand on the knob as I slide it into place, it pops open. Shutting it, I stare through his blinds to make sure he hasn't returned. Walking around his desk, I remove the large painting of Italy off his wall to get to the safe behind it.

I turn the knob, trying a few combinations, but it doesn't open. "Damn it." I open drawer after drawer to search for numbers and look under each one of them. "What else could it be?" I scratch my head, then it hits me. I dial in my mother's birthday, and it opens. "Son of a bitch."

Taking out his journal, I place it on his desk and turn on the small gold desk lamp and sit in his chair. I spend the next several hours reading accounts of every transaction he's ever made with a list of names. Flipping the pages, I search for the date my mother was killed. My heart thuds when I see a name written in blue ink followed by a dollar amount with my mother's name in the memo. Balance to be paid when the job is completed. Scrolling down the page, there's an addendum. Paid in full.

"I knew it!" I slam my fist on the desk. Hot tears spill down my face, snapping pictures of the journal. I place it back in its place in this safe and shut it, carefully positioning the picture exactly where it was hanging. Once I've checked to make sure all his drawers are closed, I lock his door and shut it, pinging Luca as to where I'll meet him.

15 NOA

"I hope that's my sister making all that noise in my kitchen." Sofia stalks into the room. "Or else I may have to shoot you." She laughs.

"Hey." I walk over and hug her.

"You got some sun."

"I did."

I drop my arms, and she strolls around me, taking down a glass from the cabinet. "Are you going to tell me what you were really up to? I know you didn't go to Essex," she glances over her shoulder.

I take a seat at the bar and scoot the salad I made in front of me and pick up my fork. "I spent the weekend with Ever."

"I thought you said that was a onetime thing?"

"It was supposed to be…"

She whips around. "You have that look in your eye."

"What look?" I scrunch my nose.

"You really like him." She points.

I can't keep from smiling. "I do. For the life of me, I don't understand why Drake or Bruno have a problem with him."

"Are you sure you're not blinded by hot sex?" she snickers.

"The sex is amazing, but I've gotten to know him, and he's charming, smart, and romantic. He has his secrets, but so do I. I haven't been an open book with him either."

"You don't have secrets. You have trauma. There's a difference." The ice clangs in her glass as she fills it from the fridge.

"He's had his share of trauma too. You should see the scars on his back."

"Scars?"

"Crap, I shouldn't have mentioned it."

"Well, you did, and now you have to give me details."

"The only thing he told me was that his father caused them. He didn't say why or how, and honestly, something that painful, I wouldn't discuss either. I don't talk about the night Drake was murdered."

"I see your point. I don't think, per se, that Drake had an issue with Ever. I don't believe he started coming around until after Drake was gone. It's the men he keeps company with that are the problem. Have you asked him about them?"

My finger taps my lower lip. "He gave me a nonanswer as to who they were. He did, however, give me good professional advice on how to negotiate the terms of our loan. I'm going to call tomorrow to set up a meeting."

"What are you going to do about Drake's son?"

"I was going to go there before I came here, but I changed my mind. I want to meet them in a public setting, so I called Gia and asked if we could have lunch tomorrow and to bring her sister along."

"Why does she think you want her sister to join you?"

"I told her that I knew she had interned with my husband and with her recent graduation, that I'd like to celebrate it since Drake isn't here to do so."

"Ah, smart girl. Do you think you should confront her in front of Gia?"

"I think she should know. She and Bruno loved my husband very much. I'm not a saint. I want some sort of payback since I can't contend with the issue of my husband's adultery to his face. I'll have to live with the fact he cheated and bore a child. But, I'll be damned if she gets to keep his son's identity a secret."

"I'll be there to support you."

"Thanks. I'm going to need it."

"Enough serious shit. Did you do it on the beach?" She waggles her eyebrows, and I roar in laughter.

"Don't you have your own man?"

"As a matter of fact, I don't. At this moment, I'm living vicariously through my baby sister."

She comes from around the bar and drops her arm around my shoulder. "It's fantastic to see you smiling again."

"It feels good."

"So, what happens when you're done with your missions in New York? Are you considering staying for a while?"

"My stay will be extended long enough for me to sell my apartment. Speaking of selling, did you speak with your loan officer?"

She expels air with force. "I can't get enough to finance the restaurant, and I'm not going to let you sell it for next to nothing. Drake worked hard to build up his business, and you deserve fair market value for it."

"Then I'll put it on the market with a contingency that you manage the place."

She scoots out the stool next to me. "I've been giving it some thought. I'd like to open my own place. Nothing on the grand scale of The Italian Oven. More of a mom-and-pop type joint."

"Here in New York? Not to be discouraging, but the market is fierce."

"Well, if you're not moving back to New York, I don't see any sense in me staying here either. Essex doesn't have any great authentic Italian food. In fact, I was thinking maybe we could be partners."

"That's not a bad idea."

"You'll think about it?" She raises her brows.

I stick out my hand. "There's nothing to think about. I'll foot the money from the sale of the restaurant, and you can have cart blanche to run it however you see fit."

"Yes!" She squeals and almost knocks me off the stool, hugging me.

"I can't breathe," I wheeze.

"Oh, sorry. I'm just so excited. I didn't think you'd go for it."

"It's the change I need. No more moping around.

I miss Drake, and I always will, but for the first time in two years, I feel alive inside by what life has left to offer me, and I'm going to take the bull by the horns and run with it."

"And, by a bull's horn, you mean Ever's." She jabs me with her elbow.

"You're naughty," I howl.

"What I am is exhausted. I'm hitting the shower and then bed. Do you need my car tomorrow?"

"No. I'll manage without it."

"Good, because I have to leave at the butt crack of dawn. Our chef is out with the flu."

"I'll lend a hand after my lunch with Gia and Angelica."

"Night." She waves over her shoulder.

I scarf down my salad and wash my dish and sit cross-legged on the sofa and scroll through my phone. I snapped a single picture of Ever standing on the deck looking out at the horizon without him knowing about it. His cheeks are sun-kissed, and his hair is a mess blowing in the wind, yet he still looks polished in his jeans and plain white T-shirt with bare feet.

"How have I fallen for him so easily?" I trace the picture with my finger. "Please be the good man I think you are. You've awoken the woman in me that's been drowning in sorrow." I close my eyes, recalling every detail of our weekend. I could've stayed on that yacht for a lifetime with him, escaping the reality that faces me. Even if our lives never cross paths again, I'll always be grateful for our short time together.

As if he knows I'm thinking about him, his number flashes on my phone. "One of your talents must be mind reading. I was just thinking about you."

"I couldn't end my evening without speaking to you again." His voice is deep, with a hint of sadness to it.

"Are you alright?"

He clears his throat. "Yeah, just a rough ending to my day, but now you've fixed it."

"Do you want to talk about it?"

"What I want to do is hold you."

"Where are you?"

"Parked in front of your sister's apartment."

I jump to my feet and look out the window. He's leaning against his car with his feet crossed at the ankles peering up with the phone crushed to his ear.

"Do you want to come up?"

"Yes." He disconnects, pushes off the car, and saunters to the building.

I stand with the door open waiting for him. I don't want to disturb Sofia. The elevator pings, and the doors open. His hands are tucked in his pockets, and he looks like a lost boy.

"Come here," I say, opening my arms.

He doesn't hesitate to fold me into his.

"I know you said you're alright, but your eyes are telling me a different story."

"I'd like to spare you the details and just hold you."

I take his hand and lead him into my bedroom, shutting the door behind us.

"Take off your clothes," he says. "I want to feel you against me naked."

By the look on his face, I can tell it's something he needs from me. I strip and climb into bed. He removes his clothes, and the mattress dips with his weight crawling next to me. He positions me so that my back is to his front, and he cradles me in his arms.

"Everything is good now," he whispers, kissing the back of my head.

I don't ask him any more questions. It isn't long before I hear his breathing slow down and feel the soft rise and fall of his chest. Whatever is eating at him, I'm happy that I could bring him comfort like he does me.

YAWNING, I stretch and feel the empty bed next to me. "Ever," I say softly. His clothing is gone, and for a moment, I think I dreamed him being here until I cuddle with his pillow, breathing in his scent. Glancing at the time, it's nine in the morning. This weekend must have really worn me out. I never sleep this late. Slipping on my clothes, I meander to the coffee pot. There's a handwritten note from Sofia.

I'LL MAKE *sure I have time to sit with you at lunch today.*

Love you, sis.

"I COULD USE THE SUPPORT. I'm dreading facing the woman that slept with my husband and gave him a child," I mutter to myself.

Pouring a strong cup of Joe, I dig the number out of my purse that Kip gave me and dial it.

"Leone Enterprises, how may I direct your call?"

She should answer, Mob Family, what can we take from you? "Hello. My name is Noa Sutton, and I'm the owner of The Italian Oven. I'd like to speak with Mr. Leone about an urgent matter."

"Hold, please," she says, and music blares in my ear. I pace the floor for five minutes before someone picks up.

"What can I do for you, Ms. Sutton?" The way he says my name gives me the creeps.

"Is this Mr. Leone?"

"He's my employer and has asked me to handle the situation."

I clear my throat. "I understand my late husband borrowed money from the Leone corporation."

"That's correct."

"I'd like to renegotiate the terms."

"It's nonnegotiable like we advised Mr. Oliver."

"You're a businessman. Everything is negotiable. I'm willing to give you half now and increase the interest rate for the additional monies owed for another five years."

"I guess you don't understand we won't be making a deal." His laugh borders on evil.

"I'm sorry, I didn't catch your name."

"I didn't give it."

"Perhaps you could pass on my offer to your employer."

"I'll entertain your request only because you are a striking woman."

My lungs fill with air, and I feel like my chest will explode. *He knows me?*

"Don't be so shocked, Ms. Sutton. I make it a point of knowing everyone who is in default of their loans."

"I'm not in default."

"You will be soon. I'll contact you after Mr. Leone has a good chuckle at your offer." He hangs up.

My blood boils. I hit Kip's number wanting to give him an earful.

"I'm glad you called. I hated the way things ended between us," he answers the phone.

"You won't be glad. I'm furious that you got Drake involved with the Leones!"

"Did you speak with them?"

"I spoke with someone who represented them, and he was a complete ass, and he knows who I am!" I yell.

"I told you I didn't want you to contact them. Let me try to handle it again. I'll personally go see them."

"If you don't, I stand to lose everything."

"Give me a few days."

"I'm running out of time."

"I know, I know. I'll handle it."

I hang up and curse under my breath. "I wish Drake was here. He'd know what to do." Tossing my untouched coffee in the sink, I snag my purse and head down the stairs. It's a nice day out, and the walk to the bank might give me time to cool down. I'll need to be level-headed when I meet with Angelica.

As I'm on the sidewalk, a car with dark windows slows down beside me. I can't see in, but I have an uneasy feeling about it. It rolls alongside me until I make it to the end of the block and turn right, walking into the bank. I look through the doors and see it speed off.

My hands shake the entire time I wait for a cashier's check to be printed. Taking a deep inhale, I slowly open the bank doors, and parked outside is a familiar vehicle.

"Luca," I say when he gets from behind the wheel and meets me on the sidewalk.

"Do you need a ride?"

"How did you know I was here?"

"I didn't. I was driving by and saw you walk into the bank."

A flash of something in his eyes leads me to believe he's lying, but I'm glad he's here. "I could use a lift to the restaurant if you have time."

He holds open the front door. "It would be my pleasure."

I get inside and breathe out, expelling my anxiousness. "It might have been my imagination, but I could swear I was being followed."

"Why? What happened?" He adjusts the side mirror and pulls out into traffic.

"A car slowed down beside me when I was walking and cruised alongside of me until I went into the building, and then it sped off."

"Did you get a look at whoever it was?"

"No. The windows were too dark."

"New York can be a crazy place for a single woman."

"It's pretty dangerous for a man sleeping in his bed too," I mumble.

"From now on, you call me. I don't want you walking the streets alone."

"I don't want to feel helpless."

"You're not. It's called being safe and not sorry."

His phone rings, and he turns it off speaker and answers it. "Yes. Mmm-hmmm. I understand." He disconnects the line.

It's none of my business who was on the other end, but I suspect it was Ever. "Is Ever having you follow me?" I crane my neck in his direction.

"No, ma'am."

I squint. "You lie for him."

"I'm telling you the truth. I'm not following you."

"So, you seeing me strolling the streets of Manhattan was a coincidence?"

"It was your lucky day, or should I say mine."

I bite the inside of my lip, wanting to believe him. "I appreciate the ride."

"You're welcome," he says, turning left at the light. "When you need a ride home, you know how to reach me."

"Luca, you're not at my beck and call."

"According to Mr. Christianson, I am."

"I'll have a discussion with him."

"It's really no problem at all."

"You're very kind."

He pulls up to the restaurant, and I get out. "Thank you, Luca."

16 EVER

"Luca, I need you to divert your direction and go to the location I pinged you. My security team called and said that a car was following Noa. Make whatever excuse you have to, but don't let her stroll the streets by herself."

"I'm five minutes from her, sir."

"Take her wherever she wants. I'll call a cab."

"Yes, sir," he says.

I call for a ride, then grab my keys and head to the locker I keep at the marina and take out all my old files on my mother's case and stash them in my briefcase.

The cab is prompt. "Where to?"

"The police department," I tell him and flip through the pictures I took on my phone of my father's notebook. I'm one hundred percent sure he killed her, and this should be enough evidence for them to reopen her case. Glancing at my watch, Luca should've reached Noa by now. I dial his number.

"Do you have her?"

"Yes," he answers.

"Keep an eye on her and make sure you're not being followed."

"Mmm-hmmm. I understand."

I disconnect. I need to find out who is tailing her and put a stop to it. If she's in danger because of me, I'll never forgive myself.

"We're here," the cab driver states, pulling directly in front of the police station.

I hop out and march inside. "I'd like to speak with the chief of police," I tell the lady at the front desk.

"Let me see if he's available. May I tell him your name?"

"Ever Christianson."

She hits a number on her phone and tells him. "He said he'll be right out."

"Thank you." I wait a few feet from her.

"What can I do for you, Mr. Christianson?" A tall man wearing a badge with the name Carmichael on it strides toward me.

"I have a matter I'd like to discuss with you in your office."

"Right this way," he says, and I follow him.

He sits behind his desk, and I stand, laying my briefcase on his desk. "I have an old case I'd like reopened." I hand him the file, and he skims it.

"This was originated in Florida many years ago."

"Yes, and the investigation was shut down before it even started. My father is the one who killed my mother."

"Aren't you Carmine Leone's son?"

"Yes." I show him the snapshots on my phone. "Here's my proof."

"I can write up your complaint, but it's not going to go anywhere."

"I'm offering you proof. He needs to be arrested for the murder of my mother."

"It's not going to happen."

I'm taken aback by his words. "Are you afraid of my father?"

He stands. "Look, son. Why don't we pretend you never came in my office today? Your father would not be happy about it, and I don't want any bloodshed on my hands."

"He has you in his pocket," I snarl.

"Call it what you will, but I know my place when it comes to the Leone family."

"Shit!" I frantically gather up my file.

"I'd burn those papers if I were you," he utters. "Like I said, I know my place, but it doesn't mean I like it or your father. I'm not going to tell him you were here or what you have on him."

I storm out and burst through the doors, leaning over and pressing my hands to my knees, trying to catch the breath that was just knocked out of me. "Damn it," I cry with warm tears streaming down my face. I knew my father's name was powerful, but just how deep, I had no idea. No wonder he gets away with murder. He pays the police to look the other way.

I stand, feeling defeated by him again. I'd take another beating from him as opposed to how I feel now. I have the proof, and there's nothing I can do about it. My feet slap the concrete hard with no particular direction in mind. I loathe my family and what I've become because of him.

"I'm sorry, Mom," I whimper. "All the things you taught me got buried in the beatings. I'm so, so sorry."

I walk several miles and find myself outside of my father's building. Biting the inside of my cheek so hard it draws blood, I bound through the doors and storm into his office. Victor's head spins around, and then he stands, pulling his suit jacket together.

"I'll inform the client of your answer," he tells my father.

"Tell our client I expect payment in full with no delays," he growls.

Victor looks me up and down before he exits the office.

"You look like shit," my father says.

"You killed her, and I know it."

He walks by me and shuts his door. "Which she are we referring to?"

"You bastard. You killed my mother."

"You have no proof," he says and saunters to his chair.

I can't tell him I do because then he'll know I broke into his safe.

"Just admit it!" I fume.

"This notion that I killed your mother—is that why you've rebelled against me all these years?"

"I've defied you because you've turned me into something I'm not!"

"You can hide behind your mother's last name all you want. You're a Leone, and it's about damn time you live up to your family name."

"I don't want to be like you or have anything to do with you. I just as soon see you dead!"

"Watch it, boy," he snarls, aiming a finger at me.

"Why did you kill her?" I glare.

"Sit." He points.

Reluctantly, I take a seat.

"Your mother was the sweetest thing I'd ever met in my life. Very naive and innocent to who I was, but I had to have her. I loved her so much that I tried to give up this life, but it kept sucking me back in. Your mother walked in at a very inopportune time. She saw something she shouldn't have, and she threatened to call the cops. I calmed her down. At least, I thought I did. The next thing I knew, she emptied out one of my bank accounts and disappeared along with you in her belly."

"You didn't give her enough credit for being smart. She was able to dodge you for years," I snap.

"Believe it or not, I loved her. Unfortunately for your mother, when I found her, she refused to hand you over to me. I begged her to come back and give us another try."

"She must have really hated you."

"She left me no choice."

I lunge over the desk, getting my hands around his throat. "I fucking hate you!"

I hear the door fly open, and two of his security guards are prying my fingers off him. One holds my arms behind my back, and the other one punches me repeatedly, alternating between my face and my gut.

"That's enough!" my father barks, and the beating stops. "Get him the hell out of my office. Don't come back until you've licked your wounds and decided to accept your family position."

"I'll never come crawling back to you," I rant over my shoulder as they're hauling me out of his office and tossing me on the street.

17 NOA

"Do you think this table is okay?" I ask Sofia.

"Yeah, I didn't want one out in the open area. I think tucked in the corner of the bar is the best choice."

"They should be here any minute." I wring my hands together.

"Breathe. I know this will be difficult for you, and honestly, I can't say that I don't want to choke her for you, but you're doing the right thing with the boy."

I inhale sharply when I see Gia holding Drake's son on her hip with Angelica trailing behind her. Bruno brings over flutes of champagne to celebrate. I feel bad because they have no idea what I'm about to expose.

"It's so nice to finally meet you, and thank you so much for doing this for me." Angelica holds out her hand, and I stare at it for a moment until Sofia nudges me.

"Thank you for accepting the celebration lunch." It sounded even mechanical to me, but I wasn't expecting her to be nice.

They all find a seat around the table, and I can't help but stare at Drake's son.

"This is my adorable nephew, Milo," Gia says, snuggling him against her cheek.

"I've taken the liberty of ordering us appetizers," I say. My gaze shifts from the boy to the woman my husband had an affair with. She's pretty and a few years younger than me. My gut ties in knots thinking about him touching her, kissing her…

"I'd like to propose a toast," Bruno blurts out. "To the next greatest chef in New York." We all tip our glasses.

"Your husband was a remarkable teacher." Angelica plasters on a smile.

I bet he was. "He loved the restaurant business."

"I want you to know how sorry I am for your loss. He was an amazing man."

Does the cheating bitch have any sense of guilt for

screwing around with another woman's husband? I want to choke her.

Sofia kicks me underneath the table.

"He was a good husband, so I thought…"

Gia frowns and tilts her head. "Noa," she says.

I take a deep inhale. "I've recently come to find out that Drake had an affair." My harsh stare points at Angelica, and she nervously swallows.

"That's not true. Drake adored you." Bruno half laughs.

"Whoever told you that is a liar," Gia balks at my statement.

"Tell them, Angelica, or I will." Daggers fly from my eyes to hers, my teeth grinding.

"What's she talking about?" Gia twists to face her sister.

"Let me take the boy." Bruno gets him free of Gia's arms and walks a few feet away but remains in earshot.

Angelica presses her lips together and defiantly juts her chin. "How did you find out?"

"He kept a journal that I was unaware of until a few days ago."

"You slept with Drake?" Gia's voice raises, filling the room, and heads turn in our direction.

"Neither one of us meant for it to happen. He was lonely, and I adored him."

"I can't believe this!" Gia tosses her hands in the air.

"There's more," I say, angling my head to the side.

"What more could there be? You slept with one of my best friend's husband!"

"Kip told you, didn't he?" Angelica's lip quivers.

"Kip told her what?" Bruno returns to the table.

Angelica casts her gaze downward. It's not because she's sorry for sleeping with my husband; she's only sorry that the truth is about to smack them all in the face.

"Milo is Drake's son," I finally say the words out loud, and it rips my heart to shreds. *She gave him something I never did.*

Gia gasps. "All this time, you lied!"

"I couldn't tell you. I knew how angry you'd be." She touches Gia's arm, but she jerks it away.

"I'm going to take Milo to my office. He doesn't need to hear any more." Sofia stands, and Bruno hands him to her.

"I felt sorry for you and supported you. You said the father of the child wanted nothing to do with him. That's not the type of man Drake was," Bruno barks.

"He wanted to tell you, and I begged him not to. I knew how close all of you were, and he was a good man. He ended our affair, but he didn't turn his back on his son. He deposited money in my account every month to support him."

"That part is true," I add. I dig in my purse and take out the cashier's check. "As devastated as I am that the man I loved cheated on me, he produced a son, and I know he'd want his future to be secure." I slide the check across the table. "It's the money I received from Drake's life insurance policy. He'd want Milo to have it." I resolved to do this, but I'm struggling because it could pay off part of the debt that's owed. In my heart of hearts, I know Drake would lose this place before not supporting his child. I'll figure out something. "If he didn't have a son, this conversation would have gone very differently." I let out some of my anger behind gritted teeth.

Gia pops up from her chair and hugs me. "I'm so sorry. I had no idea."

"I know you didn't."

"I would have told you had I known, and I would've kicked Drake's ass." Bruno has his hands on my shoulders.

"I wish he was here so I could do it myself."

"I can promise you one thing, now that I know

the truth, Milo will know his father was a decent man." He snarls his lip at Angelica.

"Honestly, I'm relieved it's all out in the open. I want my son to know who his father was." Her eyes fill with tears for the first time as she looks at me. "Drake did love you more than you know. He felt so guilty for what we had done."

"You knew he was married, and regardless if he was lonely or not, he wasn't yours to have! He was my husband, and you've taken something precious away from me. And as much as I've fought it, it's tainted my memories of him. If these two weren't my friends, this conversation wouldn't have been so civil." I exhale. "Just promise me you'll take good care of his son."

"I will." Tears pool down her face as she nods. "And I am sorry we hurt you, but I'll never regret having his son."

"If you'll excuse me, you'll have to enjoy your meal without me. It's on the house." My legs want to give away when I stand, but I'm determined not to let her see me falter. I make it into Sofia's office before my unshed tears reign down. She scoots out with the child and then rushes to my side.

"I'm so proud of you." She hugs me, keeping me

from going to my knees. "If it were me, I'd have plucked every hair out of her head."

"He has Drake's eyes," I cry.

"You're going to be okay. I promise." She runs her hands through my hair.

"It hurts so bad." I bury my face in her neck.

Bruno bursts into the office, and the tears in his eyes equal mine. Sofia steps aside, and he replaces her in my arms. "You're a damn good woman, and I'm sorry they hurt you. If Drake were alive, I'd punch him in the dick."

I glance at Sofia. "I'm going to be okay," I bravely sniff, repeating her sentiment.

"Gia feels horrible." Bruno shrugs a shoulder to wipe his tears.

I extend my arms and grip his biceps. "She shouldn't. It wasn't her fault, and if anything good has come of this, it's the fact that the two of you will be in his son's life, and for that, I'm grateful."

"After everything that you've been through…"

I press my fingers to his lips. "Right now, I can't focus on anything but moving forward. I don't want my love for Drake to turn to anger, and neither should you. He made a mistake. I will always remember him as the first man I ever loved besides my father, and I'll find a way to forgive him."

"I'll respect you and forgive him too."

"Thank you." I kiss his cheek. Taking a step back, I grab a tissue off of Sofia's desk and blow my nose. "No more tears. What's done is done."

Bruno's head bobs, and he walks out. I shuffle into the bathroom and wash off the mascara that's smeared down my face.

"You don't have to stick around and help out. Why don't you go take a walk in the park, or go shopping and buy something that will make you feel better." Sofia sticks her head inside.

"I want to help." I dry my face. "I need to help because the other thing on my list to do today will only make me sadder. I can't think about selling the apartment. It will have to wait another day or so."

"Alright then. Do you want to work in the kitchen or on the floor?"

"I'll mingle with the customers and help out the wait staff."

"Good. If at any time you change your mind, just let me know, and I'll get it covered."

"Is she gone?" At this moment, I can't say her name.

"Yes. Gia took them home."

"Then let's get to work."

I walk out to a restaurant packed full of people

knee-deep on a waiting list and dive right in helping out. One of the waitresses is struggling with a difficult table, and I send them a round of drinks on the house, and it settles them down. After they leave, she tells me thank you and says they left her a note of an apology and a generous tip.

I shuffle food and drink trays and take time to mingle with a few of the customers like Drake used to do. He said taking the time with people is what made him so successful.

On my trip to the bar to pick up some drinks, the man that was in here before with one of Ever's table buddies is sneering at me. He watches me, and my stomach rolls when he licks his lips, eyeing my breasts. I get Bruno's attention and lean over the bar. "How long has the guy at the end of the bar been here?"

"Too long, as far as I'm concerned. I can have him removed."

"He's giving me the creeps."

"Say no more." He tosses his hand towel on the counter and struts over to him. I can't hear what's being said, but the man shifts his gaze around Bruno and curls his lip. Bruno's arms cross over his chest, widening his stance, and the man sizes him up. He must consider him a threat because he shoves the stool, knocks it over and tosses cash on the counter. He eyes me until he's out the front door.

"Thank you," I mouth to Bruno and take the drinks to the table.

The lunch crowd rolls into dinner chaos, and I'm thankful because by the time I fall into my bed, I'm exhausted and have had no time to digest what happened today.

Checking my phone, I'm disappointed there have been no texts from Ever today. I ring his phone, and it goes straight to voicemail.

"Hey, I just wanted to hear your voice, and I was hoping you'd be outside my window again. Call me."

TWO DAYS HAVE PASSED, and I haven't spoken to or heard from Ever. Perhaps he's changed his mind about what he wants from me. I've put off listing the apartment long enough, and I want Ever to handle it for me. Or maybe it's an excuse to see him again.

Sofia drops me off at the Ritz-Carlton on her way to work. The doorman greets me, and I go directly to the man managing the elevators.

"I'm here to see Mr. Christianson," I say.

"I'm sorry, ma'am, but he no longer resides here," he tells me politely.

"Where did he go? Does Luca still live here?"

"I'm not at liberty to say. You're welcome to speak with the manager."

"No. It's okay," I say, walking away dumbfounded. Not only did he change his mind, he moved. An ache builds in my heart, not of longing but of fear as I make my way down the sidewalk. What if something happened to him. I step to the side and take out my phone, calling Ever's number again, only to be greeted with another recording. I hang up and dial Luca's number.

"Ms. Sutton," he answers.

"Luca. I've been trying to get a hold of Ever for a couple of days, and I went by the hotel. They said he's no longer living there."

"That's correct."

"What's going on? Where is he? Is he alright?"

"Give me a second," his voice deepens, and I can hear him walking. "I'm breaking a confidence in telling you this, but he's in bad shape. He received some disturbing news, and he's not handling it well. I can't get into the specifics of it, and he asked me not to call you, but in my humble opinion, he needs you."

"Where is he?"

"The yacht."

"You're with him?"

"Yes, I haven't left his side."

"I'll hail a cab and be right there. Don't tell him I'm coming."

"I won't. But I want to prepare you. He's not going to be happy when you see him."

"It's okay. I'll handle it, but thanks for the warning."

I hang up and spin on my heels to get a cab, and the man that Bruno tossed out of the bar is in my face. "Noa Sutton," he spats my name, and my eyes bulge, recognizing his voice from my phone call to the Leone Organization.

"Why are you following me?"

"I wanted to tell you face to face that my boss had a good belly laugh at your offer, and I'm here to remind you the money is due in full within one week."

"I've already told you I don't have that kind of money."

"Then the restaurant will be ours, and I'll expect you and your staff to never set foot in the place again."

"I'm not going to let you steal everything my

husband worked for his entire adult life. I'll be contacting my attorney. You can't just bully me into something. There's a legal process, and I don't give a crap who you work for. It will be followed. My restaurant and its employees aren't going anywhere." I'm not sure where my bravery has bubbled up from, but I refuse to be walked on by anyone.

"I admire your courage, but you're playing with fire that will likely get you killed." He spits on the ground. "Have a good day, Ms. Sutton."

When his back is to me, my legs tremble, and my heart is skipping beats. I've poked the bear of the Leone family.

Hailing a cab, I urge the driver to get me to the marina the quickest way possible. While I'm in the back seat, I call the man that's handled all my husband's legal affairs and tell him what's going on. He assures me he'll delve into it and that it's not legal for them to take over the business. He tells me it's a scare tactic but that I need to be diligent with my safety because the Leone family is not one to be messed with. Their pockets run deep in Manhattan, and they've corrupted the police and have paid off a few judges.

My hands are visibly shaking when I pay the taxi driver and rush out of the car, running on adrenaline to the yacht. Luca is standing on the deck waiting for me.

"Thank you for coming. I'll say it because he won't."

"You said he's in bad shape. What do you mean?"

"He's been drinking for days, and needless to say, he's rough around the edges when he's had too much bourbon."

"Can you tell me what set him off?"

"All I can say is that it had something to do with his mother."

"Alright. Where is he?"

"Just inside these doors." He points.

18 EVER

The door opens, but I pay it no mind. Luca has been in and out several times, checking on me without saying a word. Smart man, I'm in no mood for a lecture. What I am longing for is another drink. I tip my glass to my lips and polish off the brown liquid, then stumble when I turn to pour another one. "What the hell are you doing here?" I snarl, wanting to be left alone.

"I haven't heard from you in several days, so I went to the hotel, and they told me you weren't living there anymore," Noa speaks softly, approaching me.

"Let me guess." I wave my glass in the air, "Luca told you where to find me, and I bet he said I needed help," I shout loud enough for him to hear me outside.

"Do you? Need help?" She steps closer.

"What I need is to be left alone!"

"To wallow in self-pity?"

Her words piss me off. "You have no idea what my life has been like!" I push past her and clang my glass on the bar, knocking it over. "Shit!" My world spins as I reach over to grab a towel to clean what spilled out of the glass.

"Let me help you," she utters, rushing to my side.

"Why are you here? You and I were nothing more than a few nights of sex," I slur.

"I don't believe that, and if you were sober, you wouldn't either. I'm here because I care about you, and you're obviously hurting."

I snatch a bottle of bourbon. "That's what this is for. It numbs the pain."

"What happened with your mother?"

"Damn you, Luca. You're fired!" I yell at the top of my lungs and stumble, falling to the ground.

Noa picks up the bottle of bourbon and pours it down the drain.

"Stop!" I stagger and fail to get to my feet.

"I'm not going to let you kill yourself drinking." She continues emptying the bottles.

"You're not my mother!" I yell, then curl into a fetal position. "I'm so sorry," I cry. "I couldn't save you."

My eyes are closed, but I can hear her feet slapping the floor, and the next thing I know, she's sitting with me, cradling my head.

"Please let me in. Tell me what happened," she coos softly, running her hand through my messy hair.

My chest burns to tell her, and I retch through my words. "He killed her," I sob.

"Your mother? Who killed her?"

"My father!" My shoulders bounce with my cries.

She gasps and positions herself in my arms, holding on tight.

"I have the proof, but there's nothing I can do about it."

"Did you go to the police?"

"Yes, and he's lined their pockets so they'd look the other way."

"I'm so sorry, Ever." She repeatedly kisses my face, and I clutch to her like a lifeline.

I've never needed anyone…but her. She's the one good thing that's happened to me in my life, but in my heart I know I'm not good for her. I'll only bring her more heartache. "You have to go." I push her away.

"I'm not going anywhere until I know you're okay."

I push off the ground and wobble to my feet. "I'll only hurt you in the long run."

She meets me on her feet. "I'm willing to risk it."

Her eyes are soft and beautiful. I can't handle the way she's looking at me…like she loves me. Nobody has ever loved me since my mother died. I take her by the arm. "You have to leave. It's for your own good."

She jerks free, and I grind my teeth, but she doesn't budge. "I'm not leaving you like this. If when all is said and done, and you don't want me in your life, I'll go, but until you've sobered up and can think straight, I'm going to be your worst enemy."

She crosses her arms over her chest, and I burst out laughing. "God, you're beautiful and fierce."

Luca pops his head in the door. "Is it safe to come inside?"

"I fired you!" I snap.

"He's not fired," Noa snarks, and I'm turned on by her sexy mouth. "Help me get him in the shower," she orders Luca.

"I'd rather take you to bed," I quip, waggling an

eyebrow; at least, that's what I think I'm doing. The room is fuzzy, and my stomach is rolling. My head spins with each step. "I don't feel so good." I belch.

They escort me faster into my cabin and then rush me into the bathroom, where I barely make it in time to vomit up days of drinking on an empty stomach. I retch repeatedly. I hear the shower running, and then a cool compress is laid on my forehead.

I clutch the porcelain and heave again until there is nothing left.

"You good?" Luca asks.

I nod and use the towel bar to help balance me to my feet.

Noa works on unbuttoning my shirt.

"I get to undo yours next." I grin.

"Okay, Casanova," she snorts.

"I love when you make that cute little sound." I touch her lips.

"Why don't you let me undress him?" Luca asks.

"She's way prettier," I slur, and he ignores me peeling my shirt off, and then goes for the button on my jeans.

"I can do it," I bark and fumble with the button, and finally relent, dropping my hands to my side. "I give."

Noa unfastens my jeans and shimmies them down my legs along with my boxers and I step out of them and into the shower. "Shit! It's cold."

"You need it to sober you up," Luca states.

I turn the faucet to hot, and within seconds, the room steams up. The water raining down on my head feels like darts pinging on my scalp. My temples throb, and my mind rushes to the conversation with my father, taking me to my knees.

"I'll handle it from here," Noa tells Luca, and the next thing I know, she's in the shower with me, fully clothed, caressing my back. "I've got you. You don't have to go through this alone." She braces her arms underneath my shoulders, getting me upright. Lathering a washcloth, she methodically washes every inch of my body, trying to remove the pain. I've never felt such empathy and love from a woman.

"I hate the scars your father left on your back, but the ones on the inside I loathe more. You're a beautiful, broken man. You can't let him control who you are or what you're yet to become. Those choices are in your hands, Ever. Don't let him win by killing what's left in your heart because I've seen what's inside. It's unstoppable and full of love to give. He took your mother's life, but don't let him steal your memories of her and all the things she taught you."

I turn around to cast my eyes at hers. "I'm so damaged, yet you see the good in me."

She sweeps my wet hair out of my face. "That's what you've shown me."

"What if I'm as evil as him?" My bottom lip trembles.

"You're not, Ever. There's too much of your mother in you to ever be evil."

"I'm not worth it. You need to run as far away from me as you can before it's too late."

"You're not getting rid of me that easily."

I anchor my knuckle under her chin. "I don't want to love you, but damn it to hell, god forgive me, I do. I'm going to bring you nothing but heartache, yet I can't stop myself from feeling the way I do about you."

"We all have our demons, Ever. We'll work through them together. Now, let's get you out of here and dried off."

She strips out of her clothes, and they crumple to the shower floor. She wraps herself in a towel, and then dries my body. I walk naked behind her, and she pulls back the comforter on the bed.

"Get in," she orders.

"Not without you," I say.

"I'm not going anywhere."

I climb in and lay on my side, and she curls in behind me, laying her chin on my shoulder. "Get some sleep."

As soon as I shut my eyelids, I drift off in the comfort of her arms.

MY EYES ARE BLURRY, and my head is throbbing. I have no idea what time it is or how long I've been sleeping. My stomach growls in protest of its neglect of food. The clock flashes seven fifteen. I don't know if that's morning or night because my cabin is blacked out. What I do know is my bed is empty. I rub the scruff on my face, that's now a soft beard, and try to scratch through my foggy memories of Noa being here.

"I yelled at her," I mutter. I vaguely remember her undressing me, or was it Luca? Lord, I hope it was her. Tossing back the comforter, I untangle from the sheets to find I'm naked. Flipping on the lamp, I drag on a pair of jeans and a T-shirt, not bothering with shoes, I walk into the hallway, and the bright light blinds me. "It's morning," I mumble, squinting.

I find Luca and Noa sitting on the sofa of the main deck. "Morning," I grunt.

"You're finally awake," Luca says.

"Welcome back to the land of the living." Noa gets up and wraps her arms around my waist.

"How long have I been out?"

"A day and a half," Luca states.

"You've been here the entire time?" I peer down at Noa.

"She hasn't left since she arrived." Luca walks over to the kitchen area. "Would you like a cup of black coffee?"

"Thanks, I could definitely use it."

"I bet you're starving. I had your staff make breakfast in case you woke up. I hope it's okay."

I take a step back and run my hair through my overly long hair. "I owe you an apology. Some things are still murky in my head, but I remember yelling at you, and you didn't deserve it."

"It was the alcohol talking. Not that I'm condoning you getting inebriated, but you let it speak for you." She narrows her eyes. "Don't let it happen again," she speaks sternly.

"Yes, ma'am." I laugh and peck her lips.

"It's Luca you owe an apology to."

"You did fire me." Luca shrugs.

I let go of her and walk over to Luca. "I'm sorry.

You're my best friend, and you deserve better of me. You know I'd never fire you."

"I knew when you sobered up you'd come to your senses." He chuckles and extends his hand. "I do, however, expect a raise." He winks.

I take his hand and draw him into my chest. "Thank you for caring about me."

"You're like the son I never had."

The smell of food has me releasing him. My staff lays out a spread of food on the counter, and I waste no time diving in, stuffing half of a pancake in my mouth. "I'm so hungry," I mouth between chewing.

I pile food on my plate, and Noa puts a few pieces of fruit in a bowl. "Aren't you going to eat?" I ask Luca.

"No, sir. I have a few errands I need to run." He gazes at Noa. "I'll be back to give you a ride home."

He leaves, and we take our plates to the coffee table and sit on the floor. "I really am sorry for the things I said."

"I hope not all of them."

I shut my eyes, recalling what I voiced to her in the shower.

"I don't want to love you, but damn it to hell, god forgive me, I do. I'm going to bring you nothing but

heartache, yet I can't stop myself from feeling the way I do about you."

"I told you I loved you." I blink a few times.

"I believe the words were, 'I don't want to love you,' was more like it, but is that true, or was it the alcohol speaking for you?"

"It was the truest thing I've ever said." I draw her into my lap. "I love you, and you're the one thing I don't want to lose."

"God help me, I love you too. You notice I didn't choose the word 'forgive me' because there is nothing to forgive. There's no fighting what's between us." She sweetly kisses my lips. "You taste like pancakes." She giggles.

"I can't believe you stayed."

She edges out of my lap. "Why didn't you tell me you had moved out of the hotel? I thought you had changed your mind about me when I went there and was told you were gone."

"I'm not used to sharing my secrets with anyone, but I have a lot of them. My place was broken into while we were gone over the weekend, and it was no longer safe for me to be there."

"Who would do that?"

"The same person who is responsible for my mother's death."

"Your father?"

"Yes."

"I hope I never meet the bastard."

"Good, because I don't want you anywhere near my family."

"I came by your hotel because I hadn't heard from you, and we had discussed listing my apartment for sale. I'm ready to do that now."

"So you can go back home," I say softly.

"Yes, that's always been the plan for me to leave. But I need something in addition."

"Name it."

"You mentioned you'd be willing to let me borrow the money to pay off the restaurant's debt. I'd give you the cash we have on hand and pay you interest with the goal of paying you back with the sale of the restaurant. It's the only way I can get these men off of my back."

"Do you really want to sell it?"

"My sister wants to partner with me in opening a restaurant in Essex. So yes, I want to sell it, but I don't know how long that would take, and I only have another week to pay off the loan. The man I spoke with on the phone knows me, and he's been showing up at the restaurant. He threatened me on the street."

My security team has probably been trying to get a hold of me, and I was out of my mind drunk for days. "What did he say to you?" My blood boils.

"He told me his boss had a good laugh at my offer and then warned me that I was playing with fire and that it would likely get me killed if I didn't cooperate. I can't risk my sister's or my employees' lives. That's the only reason I'm asking you for a loan. I know it's against all the rules to mix business with pleasure, but I'm getting desperate."

I lay my hand on her thigh. "It's my pleasure to help you. Have Sofia send me everything you've received from them, including the original signed loan. I'll take care of everything, and we'll work out the details later. I've worked for men like them. Trust me when I tell you they follow through with their threats, but I'm not going to let anything happen to you." I caress her cheek.

"I do trust you." She leans into my touch. "I'm glad you're better, and I understand all too well how it feels to not get justice for someone murdering the person you love. It's been a difficult journey, and I know how much you want justice. It's what I've craved every day since Drake was taken from me, but I've learned to live with the fact that his killers may never be found and brought to justice. It almost seems like a lifetime ago. I've had to convince myself I couldn't quit living because he did."

"You've never told me the details of that night."

She lifts her wrist, looking at her watch. "My story will have to wait for another day."

We both get to our feet. "Thank you for setting me straight."

"You're welcome, but you may have to return the favor one day when I lose my shit." She stands on her tiptoes and kisses my chin. "I like the beard."

"Do you now?" I purr. "We'll have to test it out to see how well you like it."

"Are you teasing me with a good time?" her eyes sparkle.

"I'm not the type of man that teases. A promise."

"I better get out of here before I never, *ever*, leave your bed."

"Nice play on words." I chuckle. "Aren't you supposed to wait on Luca to drive you around? I'm not comfortable with you walking the streets of Manhattan until we get the loan settled."

"I texted Sofia. She's picking me up."

"You told her where I live?" My tone is gruff.

"Yeah…I didn't know your whereabouts were a secret."

It just may have put all of our lives in danger. "I'd rather not give my father a way to find out."

"He still lives in New York?" She juts her chin.

"Unfortunately, yes."

"I'll have a talk with Sofia and ask her not to tell anyone, not that she would anyway, but just to be on the safe side." Her phone pings. "She's waiting. Call me later, and if you don't, I'll hunt you down." She smiles.

"Hey." I snag her hand. "How did your lunch meeting go?"

"It's all done as far as I'm concerned. Drake's child will be taken care of, and I'd like to forget the rest of it."

19 NOA

"Is Ever alright?" Sofia asks before she turns out of the marina parking lot.

"He was in pretty bad shape. I've never met someone so broken from the hands of his own family." I angle toward her. "Speaking of which, please don't tell anyone where Ever is staying. He doesn't want his father to find him."

"I promise I won't say a word, but do you think your safety is in jeopardy by being involved with a man like him?"

"A man like him," I repeat her words. "I thought I was safe with someone like Drake, and look how that turned out. Not only did I almost die, he broke my heart in the end."

"I know, but I don't want to see you hurt again."

"I'm not going to live inside a bubble any longer. Ever makes me feel things I'd long forgotten and, on some level, never knew existed. I've not been one to take chances, and by no means have I been risky with my heart, but there's something about him that makes me want to give him every part of me."

"I hear a but in your tone." She takes her eyes off the road to look at me for a second.

"He's essentially been a loner, and he has some self-destructive tendencies that mask his emotional pain. He punishes himself for not being able to save his mother. Despite all of it, I see a desirable man who is worthy of being loved."

"Honestly, it scares me. Perhaps you should heed the warning from Bruno."

"Do you think if I thought Drake's life was in danger that I wouldn't have loved him?"

"The difference is, Ever is the danger. Drake would never have purposely put you in harm's way."

"He's not the man you think he is. I'm not going to walk away from him because his father is a monster. Ever is worth it, and I've fallen wildly in love with him. Don't ask me to explain how it happened so quickly." I wave. "I feel like he's what I've been missing my entire life, and I didn't know that I'd been lacking for anything. If my heart belonged to Drake, then why didn't I give up everything to be with him? I can't put all the blame on him for the affair. I was never home. If I'm truly honest with myself, I kept him at arm's length because he took me to a place I didn't want to be. New York was never my lifestyle, but it was his, and he loved it. In essence, both of us chose our careers over loving each other."

"So, this thing with Ever, you're going to stay in New York?"

"No. My heart will shatter in a million pieces when I leave him, but I wouldn't give up my experience with him for all the money in the world. He's healed me, and even though I love him, I know I can stand on my own two feet and stop burying my head in the sand. As much as it pains me, our lives are worlds apart." I say these words to my sister, making it sound so simple as my heart is wrecked with the idea of walking away from him. He was never in my plans when I came here, but he crashed into my life with such an unexpected vengeance that he took my breath away, even from the first moment I laid eyes on him sitting at the bar.

"I'm grateful to him for helping you move on with your life."

My phone vibrates, and I blush when I read a text from Ever.

I miss you already and want to do all sorts of naughty things with you.

And, as if he heard our conversation, he adds:

Please don't ever leave me. I don't think I could live in a world without you in it now that I've found you. You make me want to be a better man. I'll give up my entire world for you, and follow you anywhere.

My heart thuds with love for this man. Before I can type a response, my phone rings with Kip's name popping up.

"Hey."

"I need to speak with you in person." His voice is rushed. "Meet me at my house."

"Can't we just discuss whatever it is over the phone?"

"No. I found out who killed Drake."

"What?" I gasp. "Tell me!" I demand loudly.

"What's going on? Who's on the phone?" Sofia swerves off the road.

"I will tell you everything, but not over the phone. I'm texting you my address," he says and doesn't give me time to respond when he hangs up.

My hands shake as I read the address to Sofia.

"Take me to Kip's house." I show her the information.

"Not until you tell me what's going on."

"Kip said he knows who killed Drake, but he can't tell me over the phone." My lip quivers.

She shoves the car into drive and makes a U-turn, squealing the tires on the asphalt. "Should we call the police?"

"No. Let's wait and see what he found out."

I send a text to him telling him we are on our way.

"Damn it! Traffic is at a standstill." Sofia tries to maneuver around cars. Horns blow, and middle fingers fly in the air as she inches past them.

My insides are shuddering more than my hands. How did he find them? What kind of danger did he put himself in to gain the knowledge?

Sofia slaps the dashboard when a delivery truck turns in front of us, blocking her path.

"I could walk faster than this," I mutter, peering at the traffic backed up.

"According to the directions you gave me, it's two miles before the turn, and then his house is another half mile down the road."

I unbuckle my seat belt. "I'm going to run."

"I don't want you going alone."

"You can meet me there when you can get through this traffic."

"At least swap shoes with me. You can't run in those babies." She points to my sandals. She shoves the car into park and removes her tennis shoes, giving them to me. I swap mine for hers and take off in a jog down the sidewalk. I'm thankful for the long runs on the coastline I'd do every morning back home, or I'd be dying within minutes.

As I make my way down the street, I see the accident that's caused the pileup, and drivers are rubbernecking as they pass, slowing traffic even more. I make the right turn and go another half mile before I see the secluded neighborhood and find the house number. It's a long driveway leading up to a modest size home. I halt on the porch when I notice the front door is ajar, and there's a video camera mounted above it dangling from its wires.

"Kip," I say, my heart beating wildly. Cautiously, I step inside. "Kip." I call his name again. I hear a noise coming from another room. Keeping my eyes open wide and padding across the floor until I come to an open room, I see a hand sticking out on the tile from behind a kitchen island. I recognize his watch and rush over to him. Blood is pooling around him, and he's lying facedown, bringing back nightmares of the night Drake was killed.

"Kip!" I holler, rolling him over. He's pale with bluish lips gasping with a gunshot wound to the chest.

He gurgles, and blood spews from his mouth. I snatch my phone from my pocket and dial 911. "Who did this?" I ask before the operator picks up, then I lay the phone down to hold pressure on his chest.

"Drake," he rasps his name. "He was…" He coughs up blood and splatters it on my arms and face.

"He what?" I cry. "The person that killed Drake—is that who shot you?"

He barely gurgles yes, then his eyes roll back in his head, and he gasps his last breath.

"No!" I scream and rest back on my knees, with my hands covered in blood.

"I got here as quick as I could," Sofia says, storming into the room, then shrieks, covering her mouth. "Is he dead?"

I nod.

She picks up my phone, hearing the 911 operator on the other end asking if I need help. Her voice quivers, telling them the address. She keeps the line connected as she paces and pushes the phone away from her ear. "Did he tell you who did this?"

"He tried," I weep.

"Maybe he wrote down what he knew on paper." She starts rummaging through his kitchen and living room.

"Quit touching his things. We need to let the police handle it." I slowly get to my feet.

"Whoever did this killed him for what he knew," she snaps. "Your life could be in danger!" Her eyes grow wide. "How do you know the killer isn't still in the house?" she whispers.

The realization of her words hit me. I came inside without a second thought. She jerks me by the arm, pulling me outside of the house, and within minutes, blue lights are buzzing all around us. They enter with guns blazing and search the entire house from top to bottom, not finding anyone.

We're both questioned for hours on end. When they've decided that our stories are true and are letting us go, I check my phone to see frantic messages from Ever because I haven't responded to any of his texts.

"Come on, let's get you home and cleaned up." Sofia drapes her arm over my shoulder and walks me to her car.

I lean my head on the window as she drives. "Why does this keep happening?"

"I don't know, but I hope like hell the police locate whoever did it."

"If they do, they'll have Drake's killer too."

"Kip told you it was the same person?"

"Yes."

"You're not staying in New York. It's not safe." She speeds to the brownstone. When I get out, I see Luca's vehicle parked across the street. Ever rushes in my direction and nearly gets hit by a car crossing to get to me.

"I've been calling and texting you. Are you alright?" He stops when he sees the blood stains on my hands. "What the hell? Whose blood is this?" He quickly scans my body for any injuries.

"Let's go inside, and I'll tell you what happened."

"There's no time for that. You're packing your things and going home." Sofia takes my arm and moves me toward the door of the building.

Ever follows close behind us. "Whose blood is on your hands and face?" He grinds his teeth with determination and anger laced together.

Sofia unlocks the door and pushes me inside. I wheel around to face Ever. "Kip Oliver was shot in the chest. Whoever murdered him was the same man that killed Drake."

"How…"

"He called me and said he needed to speak to me in person and that he knew who killed my husband. When I arrived at his house, his door was ajar, and his security system had been taken out."

"Was he still alive when you found him?"

"Barely."

"What did he say?" Ever braces his hands on my shoulder.

"He was spewing up blood and could hardly speak and was only able to confirm what I just told you. He spoke Drake's name, and that was it."

"I'm taking you to my place where I can keep you safe. Sofia, you're welcome to come too."

"Thanks, but I've got to go to the restaurant and take care of things."

"Do you think it's safe for you to stay here?" I hug her.

"I'll crash at Bruno and Gia's for the night. Call me in the morning." She squares off with Ever. "Don't let anything happen to her." She drills her finger into his shoulder.

"I won't. I promise."

"I'll go grab my things," I say, scooting off, leaving him with Sofia. I run into the bathroom and catch my reflection in the mirror, and my nightmare returns with flashes of Drake. I lift my hands and see the similar blood stains from that night, and I scream. "Why!"

The door flies open, and Ever is catching me before I collapse to the tile floor. "I've got you," he assures me. He strips me as I did him and puts me in the shower. He drops his clothes to the floor and gets in with me, picking up a bar of soap and scrubbing my hands and cheeks. I watch as red streams turn to light shades of pink on the shower floor.

"I'm not going to let anything happen to you. I love you," he says, piercing me with his emerald eyes.

I fold into his embrace with my body trembling, and I sob on his chest. He continues to wash me, then turns off the water, drying me off. "I can have Luca come back and get your things."

"No, I'll do it." I step out of the shower on shaky legs.

He slips on his clothes, and I get dressed. "Where is your suitcase?"

I point to the closet as I empty out the dresser drawer.

He takes my hanging clothes and runs them downstairs as I stuff my things in my bag.

Sofia meanders into the room and hugs me. "Are you sure you want to go with him?"

"Yes. I can't leave town, and I don't want to put your life in danger."

"Alright." She sighs. "Text me when you get there and call me in the morning. The police were contacting Kip's next of kin. I'll call his sister and find out when his funeral will be."

"Thank you." I zip my suitcase. "I'll want to attend."

20 EVER

I tuck her into my side, and she lays her head on my shoulder, not uttering a word on the way to the marina. Luca's eyes, heavy with worry, dart to her several times in the rearview mirror.

"She's sleeping," he whispers as he parks. "I'll get her bags."

I reach over, unbuckling her and then myself. She blinks a few times and then lies in my spot when I get out. Reaching in, I envelop her in my arms and carry her in the moonlight to the yacht. "Hold on," I say, moving up the steps. She throws her arms around my shoulders and burrows her nose against my neck until I lay her on the couch on the main deck.

"Have you eaten anything today other than the

few pieces of fruit you picked at this morning?" I push her damp hair out of her eyes.

"No. I'm not hungry. I just want to go to bed."

"You need to eat." I pick up the phone and tell my chef to prepare a warm stew. My mother always insisted a full belly would give me the energy to face all my problems. It's the only thing I know to do for her right now other than be by her side. I don't know how much more trauma she can take before it breaks her.

She sits in the corner of the couch with her legs drawn up against her chin. "Thank you."

"You don't ever have to thank me for taking care of you."

"When I told you this morning you'd have to return the favor when I lost my shit, I didn't calculate it would be so soon." She attempts a laugh.

"I'm sorry about Kip." He was playing with fire when he got involved with my father. Her words ring in my ears. *It was the same person that killed her husband.* There has to be a connection. Did Kip let Drake in on some of his investments, or did he witness something he shouldn't have?

"You should run as far away from me as you can. The men in my life seem to have the same fate."

"I don't scare off so easily." I sit facing her.

"When I saw him on the floor bleeding out, all I could see was Drake's face."

"Tell me what happened the night your husband was killed." I lay my hand on her knee, then stroke her calf, willing her to open up.

"I had come home for a long weekend, and we had been out celebrating a milestone. My food blog had been picked up by a major outlet, and it boosted my career to the next level. When we came home, we got lost in each other." She stops and looks at me.

"I get the picture. It's okay."

"The police believe the perpetrators were already inside the house." She licks her dry lips. "They were watching us. We drifted off to sleep in each other's arms, and I recall hearing a noise that woke me up. Drake jumped out of bed and pulled on his boxers, grabbing his pistol from the nightstand. He told me to stay put but call 911.

"Before I could reach for my phone, someone came out of the dark and punched Drake in the face, and they wrestled for the gun. When I scrambled out of bed, a man grabbed me from behind, covering my mouth with his gloved hand urging me not to scream. I bit hard enough through his glove for him to let go. The next thing I remember is that he was on top of me, tearing at my shirt. He hissed in my ear that I was beautiful, and watching me make love to my husband turned him on." She swallows and rubs her lips together. "The words he used were more graphic than mine."

I position my hands on either side of her face. "You're safe."

She continues. "I could hear Drake being beaten, and I knew I had to do something. With every ounce of my strength, I raised my knee hard, crushing his balls. He rolled off of me in pain long enough for me to get up. I was running toward the door when I took a hit to the back of my head. When I came to, I was frantic, met with complete silence. My head ached, and I could feel the warmth of my own blood in my hair. I crawled to my feet. That's when I found Drake on the landing."

"Come here." I drag her into my lap." Did you see their faces?"

"No. They were wearing masks, and it was so dark I couldn't even see the color of their eyes."

I want to rip whoever it was apart with my bare hands for touching her. "There were two men, as far as you know?"

"Yes."

My chef comes in with a couple bowls of stew on

a tray. "I had some left over from the other night. I hope it's alright."

"Yes, thank you."

Noa scoots out of my lap and tucks her hair behind her ears. "It smells so good. I didn't realize how hungry I was." She picks up her spoon and dives right in.

My mind is reeling, trying to make the connection between the incidents with Kip and Drake. "I know you two ladies have been through a lot today, but I'm going to contact your sister in the morning and have her send me the paperwork." If my gut's correct, I know who's behind it all. "I want to get the money handled, so it's one thing you can take off of your plate."

She sets her bowl on the coffee table and turns to face me. "Did you mean what you said in your text?"

"The part where I'd follow you anywhere?"

She nods and weaves her eyes back and forth with mine.

"Yes. I was only existing before you stormed into my life and stole my cold dead heart. I've come alive, and I don't want to live without you. Where you go, I go. If you want to travel around the world in this beast, we can do so. If you want to go back to Essex, then I'll be with you."

"How did we go from a casual hookup to this?"

"Does it matter?" I shrug. "Here we are."

She stands. "Take me to bed." Her hand extends toward mine.

Her fingers entwine with mine, and I let her lead me to my cabin. She eases out of her clothes and into my bed, folding back the comforter.

"You've had a rough day. I'd understand if you wanted to do nothing more than go to sleep."

Her gaze travels to my crotch, tenting my jeans. "You might understand, but I think you have a body part that disagrees with you."

I strip and slip in next to her. She moves on top of me, tucking my cock deep inside her, and makes love to me at her own pace. I don't interfere with what she needs because…she's what I need.

IT'S three in the morning, and I'm wide awake with Noa's face nestled against my chest, expelling slow puffs of warm air. My temples pound, not letting my mind shut off. This entire ordeal reeks of my family. My question would be, why did they kill Drake if they thought for one minute he'd default on the loan and they'd get the property for next to nothing. It doesn't make any sense. Perhaps I'm mistaken, and it wasn't them. For Noa's sake and mine, I pray I'm wrong, but my gut tells me I'm not.

Gently easing her off me, I get out of bed and tug on a pair of lounge pants, tying them around my waist. Padding out of the cabin, I make my way to my office and turn on a soft lamp rather than the overhead light, opening my laptop.

I scroll company reports to about the time that Drake was murdered and look for entries. My access is limited, and I wish like hell I could get my hands on my father's journal again. There's no mention of outside payments. A quick Google search gives me the exact date Drake died, and I'm able to tap into the police log thanks to my father's access. My breath gets trapped in my lungs as I read over the details given in the reports. It was a horrific nightmare for her, and I'm sorry her husband was taken from her, but I'm grateful she's in my bed.

I flip through the data sheet Nick fills out, logging his time and typical whereabouts. It's something my father requires of him. His time is written in with no mention of what he was doing. He left at nine p.m. and returned at one in the morning. This correlates with the timeframe of Drake's murder, but it doesn't prove anything. My father has him doing ill deeds at various times. "Please don't let it have anything to do with my family," I mumble.

"There you are. Come back to bed." Noa stands in the doorway, wrapped in a sheet, yawning.

I snap my laptop shut. "I didn't mean to wake you."

"You didn't. I don't want to spend another night alone reaching for you next to me and find the spot empty." She strolls between my thighs.

"You're so damn gorgeous." I trail my finger between her breasts. She drops the sheet and moves my laptop to the side of my desk, and sits with her legs wide open, inviting me to partake. I will give her whatever she wants from me. Rolling my chair out, I bend and kiss her belly button and dig my fingers into her hips.

"Lower," she purrs.

"Who am I not to oblige a sexy woman?" I grin and dip my tongue in her folds. She arches her back and lifts her hips, giving me full access. I lick and suck her until she's panting and screaming my name, her hand clinging to the back of my head, pushing it closer to her.

"You're way too sensitive to my touch." I chuckle and lick my way to her taut nipple.

"You have a wicked tongue," she says with

hooded eyes, breathing heavily. "I want to feel you buried inside of me."

"I don't have a condom in my office," I rasp and capture her bottom lip between my teeth. "We'll have to make our way back to my room."

"I can't wait that long." She dips her hand inside my pants and strokes me.

I growl and stand, ripping my pants below my waist and thrusting inside her with so much force it rocks the desk. She's everything to me. She erases the ugly in my life and replaces it with something I cherish. I can't lose her, and I can't tell her the truth, or she'll surely run as far away from me as she can, just like my mother did with my monster of a father.

With every drive into her, skin on skin, I claim her, or maybe it's the other way around. Either way, she's mine, and I'll keep her safe at all costs. I pump harder and feel myself on the edge of a cliff, clinging on for dear life. She sets off a firestorm of spasms around my cock, tightening, and I lose control, spilling inside of her before I can pull out.

"I'm sorry, baby," I rasp. "I got carried away."

A jagged breath escapes her lips. "I'm the one that took you there."

I cling to her, hoping we can stay this way and

somehow she can deliver me from the reality of my life, creating a new one for the two of us.

Pulling up my pants, she wraps her long legs around my waist, and I carry her back to bed. My mind eases, and I fall asleep next to her.

I wake to a rapid fire of screams echoing in the room. Noa is covered in sweat, and every muscle in her body is tense.

"Noa," I say softly, shaking her shoulder. "You're having a nightmare, baby."

Her eyes never open, but she settles down, curling into my arms.

"You're safe." At least it's the lie I'm telling myself. She may never be secure with me in her arms.

I roll to look at the clock, and it's six in the morning. I can't wait any longer. I need the paperwork from Sofia. Meandering to the top deck, I call her.

"Hello," she says groggily.

"Hey, it's Ever. I'm sorry to call you so early."

"Is Noa alright?" Her voice grows louder.

"She's sleeping. She asked me to look over the loan for the restaurant. I'm going to purchase the restaurant and pay off her debt. I need to know who the money is owed to."

"I have copies of it on my phone. I'll send it to you."

"I know it's an unreasonable time of morning, but could you do it now?"

"Sure. I'll send it as soon as we hang up. How is she really?"

"I'd say she's probably numb."

"Yeah, me too."

"Can I do anything for you?"

"You're doing it by taking care of my sister."

"I love her, and I need you to know I'd trade my life for hers."

"I believe you." She sighs.

"Stay safe, and if I can do anything for you, don't hesitate to ask." I disconnect and wait for the links to her file to pop into my messages.

I tap my phone, open the pdf, and skim to the last page. There it is in bold ink…my father's signature. "Fuck!" I yell over the railing into the morning air. "Damn you, Kip Oliver, for getting her involved with my family." She obviously has no idea, and I don't want her to make the connection between Carmine Leone and myself, but she undoubtedly will at some point.

I hustle to my office and put pen to paper, writing Noa a letter that will explain everything if things go seriously wrong. When I'm done, I knock on Luca's door.

"Good morning, sir," he answers with shaving cream on half his face and a razor in his hand.

"I need you to give this to Noa, but not until I tell you to."

"I don't understand." He scowls.

"She's going to hate me for what I'm about to do. This letter will explain everything. Make sure she has breakfast this morning, and keep her in your sights at all times. Take her wherever she wants to go and have my security team be extra vigilant."

"Am I not driving you, sir?"

"No. I'll take care of my own transportation."

I call an Uber driver and have him sit in the back of the marina parking lot with me in the back seat and wait for Noa to leave with Luca.

"You know this is costing you a lot of money for me just to be parked," the driver says, staring at me in the rearview mirror.

"I don't give a shit what it costs. I'll pay you for the entire day." I toss him ten one-hundred-dollar bills over the seat. "If that's not enough, I'll give you more."

He picks up the cash and counts them. "No, sir,

this should cover it. I'll cancel the rest of my calls for the day." He gets on his computer.

Around nine, Luca and Noa get in his vehicle, and my phone buzzes. "Good morning, beautiful," I answer.

"I thought we agreed you weren't leaving the space next to me empty anymore."

"I'm sorry, we did, but I couldn't sleep, and I needed to get some work done."

She sighs. "I have been keeping you rather busy with my issues."

"Look, I got the information I needed from Sofia. Your debt will be paid by the end of the day, and I'll contact my attorney to submit a fair market value offer on the restaurant."

"Are you sure you want to do this? I could just list it on the market. If the loan is paid in full, I'll have time to find a buyer. I don't want the restaurant to be an albatross around your neck any more than mine. It would tie you to New York. If you're free from this place and your father, we can go anywhere…together."

I hope like hell she still feels the same way after today. "I'll mull it over, but I'll at least get the loan handled."

"Thank you for helping me."

"I love you, Noa Sutton. Don't ever doubt it."

"Ditto."

"Try to stay out of trouble." I chuckle.

"You too. I love you."

I press the cell phone to my forehead when she hangs up. "Follow that car, but don't get too close," I tell the driver.

"You got it," he says, slipping it into drive.

I make a few phone calls, including one to the Leone family attorney, and access funds via an app.

She stops at her old apartment she shared with Drake and spends about an hour inside. When she returns to the vehicle, I'm surprised that her eyes aren't red and swollen from crying. She looks strong, as if she went in there to say goodbye and finally let go.

Before her next stop at a coffee shop, I see Victor fall in between us in his convertible. He parks when she does, and it sends red flags up my spine. "Stay here," I instruct the driver and skip out and stomp to his car and swing the door open, hauling him to his feet with my fist clutched in his collar.

"Why the hell are you following her?" I snarl.

"What's it to you?" He jerks free of my hold on him.

"She's off-limits to you, asshole." I get in his face.

He takes a step back and laughs. "She's the reason you've gone AWOL. Your brother is going to love this."

"If I see you tailing her again, they're going to be searching for your body in the river."

"That's more Nick's style and mine, not yours." He spits on the sidewalk.

"Try me." My jaw locks with my deadly glare.

"She is one fine piece of ass. I can understand why you'd kill for her."

My temper runs amuck, and my fist plummets into his face. He falls against his car, spitting blood from his mouth. "If you want me to quit following your girlfriend, you'll need to discuss my job duties with your brother. He's giving me the orders, not your old man."

"Just stay the fuck away from her!" I shove my finger into his chest. "I'll deal with my brother."

I stand back and watch him drive off and hustle to the Uber when Noa comes out of the coffee shop holding two cups.

Bringing up the address to my father's office, I show it to the driver. "This is where you'll take me next."

"We're not following the pretty woman anymore?"

"No!" I growl, and he heads into Manhattan to the Leone building.

Bypassing his secretary with my polished shoes slapping hard against the marble tile, I storm into his office, where he's in a meeting with Nick. "Great, just the two men I need to see. I'm purchasing the loan for The Italian Oven. Consider the debt wiped clean." The inside of my cheek hurts from gnawing on it, and I drill my hands into my pants pockets to fight the urge to wrap them around my brother's throat.

"The loan was meant to fail. I want the property." My father rests back in his chair and folds his hands in his lap, glaring at me with his usual disappointed look.

"You'll have no choice as to who pays it. The property belongs to Ms. Sutton. The loan will revert to me."

"I've gone through too much trouble to lose the property. You'll stand down," he snarls.

Nick gets to his feet. "Why would you bail her out?" He clicks his tongue. "You have a thing for her."

"No. It's the right thing to do. The woman has been through enough trauma."

Victor strolls into the office and grips Nick's shoulder. "You're right. He likes her." He dabs a handkerchief, wiping the blood on the corner of his mouth.

"What happened to you?" Nick asks him.

Victor tilts his head toward me.

"I barely know the woman. I feel sorry for her, that's all. And her restaurant is the busiest in Manhattan and will bring me a nice return on my investment."

"Profit you're stealing from me by paying off her loan." My father pushes off the desk and gets to his feet. "I drained your bank account. Where are you getting the money from?"

"I have good credit, and I borrowed it," I lie.

He laughs. "I get it now. You seduced the woman to get your hands on her property to make it all look legit." He rakes his glare at Nick. "Perhaps you should have thought of that instead."

21 NOA

"It's all been about money for you." My words are directed at Ever. Four heads spin in my direction and see me standing in the doorway to Carmine Leone's office. Shock is portrayed in Ever's eyes, but he appears to recover quickly.

"Ms. Sutton. I told you I'd be handling the loan for you. You didn't need to come here." He advances within a few steps of me.

My mouth is suddenly extremely dry. "I wanted to tell him in person that it was being taken care of." My heart jumps into my throat, recognizing the man who was following me. "You." I point at him and then stare at Ever. "You know him?"

One of the other men, who is younger than Ever,

steps toward me, smiling. "Ever hasn't shared with you our relationship." A sick smile creeps on his face.

A tingling sensation runs down my spine at the sound of his voice and the look he's giving Ever.

"Shut the hell up, Nick! I've told you. This is business, nothing more," Ever snarls between gritted teeth.

It's a lie. I can see it in his eyes. He doesn't want me tangled up with these people. He's trying to protect me, and I walked into something darker than I imagined.

"Let me formally make some introductions since the man who is bailing you out of your loan hasn't." He slaps Ever on the back, and out of the corner of my eye, I see Ever's hands ball into a fist at his sides. "I'm Nick, this man's better-looking brother, and this." He angles toward Mr. Leone. "Is our father."

"I'm Victor, but we've met." A sleazy grin rises on his lips.

Ever's head falls, and my mouth gapes. "Carmine Leone is your father? But your last name is Christianson." My voice cracks, knowing the reputation of the Leone family.

"My son took a beating for keeping his mother's last name." The arrogant bastard has pride buried in his chuckle.

I flinch at his tone. *The scars on his back.* "Is this true? Is this your family?" I gulp roughly.

"I told you he liked her," Victor chimes in. "I bet this charming fellow had your legs spread in no time. The ladies love him."

Ever tightens his jaw. "I told you, this is business. She means nothing to me other than making a profit on a piece of real estate."

My heart lunges, and bile rises in my throat, burning my tongue. This can't be happening. Did I let myself be used by him? Maybe Bruno was right, but looking at Ever and his body language, bundled with the time we've spent together, I don't believe it.

Boldly, I step around Nick and confront his father. "He's right. Mr. Christianson has been nothing but professional. We came to a mutual agreement of terms on the money the restaurant will be borrowing from him to cover your note. I made you an offer, and according to Victor, you laughed at it. So, I sweetened the deal, and your son accepted it." I stifle a choke calling Ever his son.

"I still have the right of refusal." Carmine pounds his fist on his desk.

"No, you don't." Ever moves to my side, and I can literally feel heat pooling from him. "I'm part owner in this madness, and I've already signed the contract releasing her from the loan, and it's been processed by our attorney. The monies will be transferred into her account by the end of the day."

"You quit, remember!" his father yells.

"Yes, but I knew you wouldn't have me removed as part owner because you figured I'd come crawling back to you."

"If you purchased the loan through the company, then I still own it."

"It's in my personal name, not the company's."

"Don't think for one minute I'm going to let you get away with this bullshit! That restaurant belongs to me!" He aims his finger at Ever.

"You lost this time, old man." Ever turns to face me. "Our business is done. You've accomplished what you came for. Now leave." He speaks sternly, his eyes frozen with mine with a silent plea for me to do as he says.

I extend my hand. "It was nice doing business with you."

His touch is gentle when our hands collide. "Have a good day, Ms. Sutton."

Behind him, Carmine drags Nick close to his ear and whispers something.

My chin goes in the air as I turn around, walking out as if I'm not shaken by the vastness of what I've learned. I keep my calm until I'm tucked inside the car with Luca.

"Why didn't you warn me?" My tears begin to fall.

"Of what, ma'am?"

"You knew Carmine Leone is Ever's father!"

He squirms in his seat. "It wasn't my place to tell you. It was his."

"I need some air." I kick open the door.

"Where are you going? I can't let you walk the streets by yourself. Mr. Christianson has instructed me not to leave you alone."

I slam the door and take quick strides down the sidewalk. Luca slowly rolls alongside me in the car.

A million and one things morph through my mind. Ever defied his mobster father. When did he quit working for him? Was it when I entered the picture? He tried to warn me to not get attached to him. He so much as told me he wasn't a good man.

I don't want to believe any of it. I've seen his heart, and he's nothing like his father. I stop dead in my tracks. Did the Leones have anything to do with Kip's death?

"Please get back in the car, Ms. Sutton. I don't want to lose my job."

I growl and swing the door open. "Oh, for Pete's

sake. He's not going to fire you, Luca. Drive me to the restaurant," I say, buckling the seat belt.

I gnaw on all my thoughts in silence as he drives through town. I jump out before he comes to a full stop, and I hear him holler when I slam the door. The restaurant is bustling, already filled with the lunch crowd. Bruno appears to be drowning behind the bar, but I don't stop to offer any help. I find Sofia in the kitchen prepping food.

"We need to talk."

"Can it wait?"

"No. Now." I take her by the arm and drag her into her office. "Carmine Leone is Ever's father."

"What?" Her eyes narrow.

"I just came from the Leone building, and Ever was there telling him that he loaned me the money to cover the contract."

"Wait! Why the hell did you go there in the first place?"

"I wanted the satisfaction of telling him he wasn't getting my restaurant."

"I hope it was worth it because now you've probably got a target on your head. You understand that the Leones are not a family to be messed with in this city. They pretty well own it."

"Ever is taking care of it."

"He's a Leone! You can't trust him!"

"Call me insane, but I have faith in him. He put on this act like I meant nothing to him in front of his family, but I could see right through it. He was protecting me."

She takes my hands in hers. "For your sake and mine, I hope you're right. What happens next?"

"Ever is either going to buy this place, which I hope he doesn't, or I'm selling it. Either way, you and I are getting the hell out of New York, and it can't be soon enough. I'm going to make some calls and get an interim manager for this place, and you're going to pack your bags."

"Why don't you let Bruno and Gia run it? They know this business as well as I do."

"That's a great idea. You get Bruno on board, and I'll hire someone to pack up the brownstone."

"Honestly, other than my clothes and a few personal items, everything can be sold with it."

"Good, it will make things move a lot quicker. I want us to be out of New York by the end of the week."

"Then I have a shit ton to do." She marches out.

I check my phone for any messages from Ever, and there is none. Logging onto Sofia's computer, I do some banking and shuffling of monies. The door opens, and without looking up, I think it's Sofia.

"Do you need me to help at the bar?" The sound of the door locking has my head sweeping up. "What do you want?" I gasp.

Nick saunters to the sofa and sits, crossing an ankle over a knee. "I'm not the fool you believe me to be. I saw the way you and Ever looked at one another. Your relationship was apparent. I've known him for a long time, and he doesn't connect with anyone. He's the epitome of a loner."

"You're mistaken."

"My father, for some sense of loyalty to him,"—he waves dismissively— "insists that Ever return to the fold, so to speak."

I want to scream to tell him Ever wants nothing to do with any of them, but I refrain because it will confirm his suspicion that I care about his brother if I do. "It's none of my concern who Mr. Christianson chooses to keep company with. My business with him is done."

He places both of his feet on the floor and leans on his elbows, rubbing the palms of his hands together. "I heard about your husband's best friend being shot in the chest."

My heart skips a beat because I know Ever wouldn't have told him about Kip.

"Seems the men in your life have a death wish, or at least a hit out on them. Sounds like you've been playing with the wrong crowd."

"I'm a busy woman. Just get to the point." I sound stern, but my insides are trembling.

"My point," he emphasizes the T, "is that you're likely to get Ever killed, or worse, accused of murdering Kip Oliver."

"He didn't kill him," I snap.

He taps a finger to his lip. "You're right. He's a bit squeamish when it comes to getting blood on his hands. I, however, don't have a problem with it. But you see, I have this love-hate relationship, more hate than love, with my half brother, and I'll have no problem planting his DNA at the crime scene."

"The scene has already been investigated."

"There are lots of advantages to being a Leone. One is owning the cops. All I have to do is make a simple phone call and plant the evidence, and our boy will be in handcuffs and charged with murder. I maybe could add a second murder charge with no problem."

My stomach violently rolls. "What do you mean?"

"Word has it they never solved your husband's murder."

The chair falls to the ground when I jump out of my seat. "Get the hell out of here!"

"I suggest you tear up the contract with Ever and never see him again, or I'll follow through on my threats. He can either die, be put in prison, or rejoin his family. It's totally up to you. I'll expect an answer in forty-eight hours. That should give you enough time to get your things and never return." He unlocks the door and smirks with a wave when he slams it shut.

I grab the trash can by the desk and retch. "Ever," I whimper his name.

Sofia crashes through the door. "I saw him leaving my office. What the hell did he want?" she's at my side, grasping my hair in her hands, keeping it out of my face.

"He threatened Ever's life if I follow through with the contract."

"What are you going to do?"

"End things with him, and we're getting the hell out of here." I snap a tissue off her desk and wipe my mouth.

"What about the restaurant?"

"I'm sorry. I've tried to save it. I hate losing it this

way. Gather the employees after the dinner shift and tell them the doors are closing as of tonight. I'll pay all of them three months' severance pay to hold them over until they can find another job. I don't want any of them working for the Leone family."

"I can't believe any of this is happening. Drake's gone, Kip's dead, and now we're losing the restaurant. Damn Drake for getting us into this mess."

"It was more Kip's fault than Drake's. He's the one that connected Drake with the Leones." I clutch my phone from the desk. "You handle things here. I'll go to the brownstone and start packing our things and contact a realtor to get it and my apartment on the market. I'll come back this evening to talk to the employees."

"Are you sure we're doing the right thing?"

"All I know is that I'm not going to let Ever lose his life because of me. I love him enough to let him go."

22 EVER

"Where the hell is he going?" I crane my neck at Nick, whose marching out of the office.

"He's got business to take care of for the company. Have a seat," my father orders and returns to his desk.

"Do you need me to stick around?" Victor asks.

"No, and close the door behind you."

"You should've stuck to screwing high-end call girls. That one's going to cost you. She's not much different from her husband. He stuck his nose where it didn't belong, and Nick had to handle the situation."

Shit. He's the one that broke into their house and shot him. My jaw is stern to keep from reacting.

"I said get the hell out of here!" my father yells and points to the door. He waits until Victor is out of sight before he speaks. "This nonsense is done. You'll do as your told and cancel the deal with Ms. Sutton."

"Did Nick kill her husband because of the loan?"

"No, but it worked in our favor for it to be in default."

"Why did he kill him?"

"What does it matter?" He raises a brow.

"Tell me, damn it!"

"Her husband was out for a run one night and was at the wrong place at the wrong time. He witnessed your brother throwing a body in the river. Nick chased after him in his car and caught him. Drake swore he wouldn't tell a soul, and Nick let him go. I'm the one that ordered the kill. He wasn't supposed to hurt the girl. I needed her alive in order to get her property."

My insides flinch, but I bury any physical reaction, but there's nothing more I want than to take him down. I have to be smarter than him. "That's all well and good, but I'm not canceling the contract."

He struts around the desk and leans on the edge, staring down at me. "You will, or I'll put a hit out on her and her sister. I'll have the restaurant torched with them locked inside of it. It will be a gruesome, painful death, and you'll have no one to blame but yourself."

I know he'll do it.

He pushes himself off the desk. "Not only will you do as I've said, you'll come back to work for me, or my threat still stands. I warned you that I'd take away everything you care about. Your friend Luca's life won't be spared either."

"You're a monster!" I seethe.

"I'm very well aware of that fact, and I'm good with it." His chair is in dismay when he sits. "So, what's it going to be? Your life for hers?"

I fucking hate him, and I'll find a way to take him down, but I'm not going to let him harm Noa. I love her enough to let her go…for now. I stand. "Promise me if I do this, she's free to go, and no one will harm her, or her family, or Luca."

"You have my word."

He may be ruthless, but he does what he says he's going to do. "I'll contact my attorney and retract the offer."

"I knew with a little prodding you'd come to your senses." He looks pleased with himself, and I'm disgusted. "Now that you're back on board, I need you on a job." He pulls a file out of his desk drawer. "I'll expect it handled by the end of the day."

Snatching it from his hand, I thunder out of his office and dial Luca's number as I run down the stairs. "Where is she?"

"She was at the restaurant, and I just drove her to her sister's place. Did she say anything?"

"She was very upset to find out you're a Leone, but she seemed more frantic after Nick paid her a visit at the restaurant."

"What the hell did he say to her?"

"She was pretty tight-lipped and shaken."

"I need you to come pick me up from my father's building."

"I'll be there as quick as I can, sir."

While I wait on a bench outside of the building, I make phone calls to the bank and my attorney. Luca honks the horn when he pulls up, and I hop in the back seat until we are away from the building, then I crawl in the front with him. "I can't give you all the details, but I'm working for my family again."

"Let me guess, your father threatened Ms. Sutton's life."

I tap my finger to my nose.

"Bastard," he mutters.

"I'll play his way for now, but I'm going to find a permanent way out of his clutches."

"I'll help in any way that I can. I know where some of the bodies are buried."

"He threatened to kill you, too, so I don't want to involve you in it unless absolutely necessary."

"I'll give up my life if it means you can finally be free of him."

"You're a good friend, Luca, but I'm not about to let that happen."

"Where am I taking you, sir?"

"To Noa."

23 NOA

"Yes, I'll hold," I tell the airline while I empty Sofia's drawers, packing her clothes in her suitcases. I don't want to stop, or my heart will explode. I've already buried my husband; I can't lose Ever in the same way…I won't.

I'm finally taken off hold. "I need two tickets on the redeye to Logan International. I'll take whatever seats you have left. Yes, we'll be checking luggage." He tells me the cost, and I give him my credit card information along with what he needs to book the tickets.

As I hang up, I hear the front door open, and I stand stock-still. Sofia wouldn't leave the restaurant this time of day. I scan the room for anything I can use as a weapon, then I recall Sofia telling me she keeps a gun under one of her pillows. Scrambling for the bed, I find it, and when I stand, I'm face to face with Victor pointing a pistol at me.

"I wouldn't do that if I were you," he tisks.

"What do you want from me?" I hold the gun in the air above my head.

"What I'd like is that luscious body of yours underneath mine." His gaze rakes over my body. "But that's not why I'm here."

I'd breathe a sigh of relief, but I'm terrified.

"I thought you should know before you leave town"—he points at the luggage—"who killed your husband."

My eyes bulge, and I gulp. "Who?"

"You should really be careful who you open your legs for. You never know what they are truly capable of." He brushes a strand of my hair over my shoulder.

"What are you insinuating?" I sputter as my heart flips over in my chest.

"Ever is the man that shot your husband."

"You're lying!" I scream.

"Funny how he ended up in your bed, and his guilt got the better of him, and he felt the need to bail you out financially."

My head rattles, and I blink several times. "That's not true. Ever wouldn't kill anyone."

"I hate to tell you this," he snarks, "he is a Leone, and they do what they're told to do, or there is a high price to pay."

"Ever didn't even know my husband and had no reason to kill him." I feel nauseous again.

"He didn't have to know him. Drake saw something he shouldn't have, and the Leones weren't about to let him live."

"This can't be true." My legs give way, and I ease myself to the edge of the bed.

"Oh, but it is. His loyalty will always go to his family first. You got caught in the crossfire. Good thing you're leaving town."

He turns his back to me for a moment, and I grip the gun in both hands. "Get the hell out of here." My voice wavers, but I steady my hands.

Victor glances over his shoulder. "I was just leaving anyway. My work here is done. If you ever show your face on the Leone turf again, I'll be obliged to taste that hot body of yours and then dump it in the river."

My finger is on the trigger, and it twitches to pull it. As evil as he is, I can't bring myself to do it. I go to my knees and sob. "It can't be true." My mind races to the first time I laid eyes on Ever. He was dining with his father and brother. Did he approach me because of his guilt? Could I have been that blind? I sit tall and inhale my cries. "I have to get the hell out of here." Moving from my knees to my wobbly legs, I lay the gun on the dresser and stuff items in the suitcase without folding them. Hauling another suitcase out of her closet, I finish off the last set of clothes when I hear my name.

"Noa." Ever appears in the doorway.

I eye the gun and then him. "Don't come any closer."

His lip is bloody, and his eye socket is red. "I ran into Victor in the stairwell. Did he hurt you?"

"What do you care?" I snap.

"I know from our interactions at my father's office you don't think I do, but it's far from the truth."

"What about the truth that you're the one that killed my husband!" I seize the gun and point it directly at him, my hands shaking.

"Is that what Victor told you? You don't honestly believe him, do you?"

"I don't know what to believe," I cry.

"It wasn't me. My father just told me he ordered the hit, and Nick is the one that broke into your house that night. Drake witnessed my brother dumping a body in the river, and that's why he killed him. I swear, I had nothing to do with it." He takes two steps toward me with his hands in the air. "You know me."

"Do I?" I lift a shoulder to wipe the tears streaming down my cheeks.

"Yes. I've never let anyone close to me but you."

"Are you working for your father again?"

He inhales sharply. "It's the only way I can protect you and your family from him."

Deep in my stomach, I believe him, and I relent, lowering the gun. "Nick showed up at the restaurant and said he'd either kill you or frame you for Kip's murder and Drake's death if I didn't give them what they wanted, and I had to leave for good." I fall into his arms, and he kisses the top of my head.

"You have to go for now, but I can promise you, they're going to pay for the crimes they've committed if it kills me, but I won't put you in any more danger."

"Come with me." I scoot back enough to look into his eyes. "You'll never be free from them if you stay here."

"Even if I leave, they'll hunt me down, and even

worse, they'll kill you. I'll move heaven and hell before I'd let them get their hands on you."

"So, this is it. I'll never see you again?"

"Never say never. They'll come a time that we find each other again, and when I do, I won't let you go." Our lips crash, and I taste his salty tears mingled with mine. "My highs with you were unstoppable, and I won't forget them. You own my heart, but my soul belongs to the devil and has been since the day I was born."

It guts me, but he's right; neither one of us is safe. I step out of his arms and sniff. "As much as it pains me to say this, because I won't risk my family to yours, I never, ever want to see you again, Ever."

He falters backward as if I've shot him, and he clutches his chest. "Please don't end things between us. Just give me some time to make them pay."

"As much as I love you, and God knows I do, I can't live like this. I won't know from day to day whether you're dead or alive. I've already buried a husband. I'd rather walk away loving you than see you lowered into the ground. Now, please go."

He looks like a man that's had all the wind knocked out of him, and he chokes on his words. "Goodbye, Noa."

When I hear the door close behind him, I lick my

wounds while I finish packing. After making phone calls to realtors and settling on one, I sign the contract via the computer and then call a cleaning company to take care of both of our apartments.

By now, the dinner crowd has died down, and it's near closing time. I feel awkward about it, but Luca showed up and insisted on driving me where ever I needed to go. He carried all of our bags to the trunk of his car and drove me to the restaurant.

"I'll be waiting to take the two of you to the airport when you're done."

"Thank you, Luca." I step inside, and there are only a few guests left at tables. Sofia has gathered the employees at the bar. We sip on wine waiting for the customers to be cashed out, and lock the doors behind them.

"What I'm about to tell you isn't easy for me, and it's not at all what I planned. Those doors will not open tomorrow. I will no longer be the owner of The Italian Oven. My husband made a financial decision that I couldn't work my way out of, so there will be new owners. I beg you not to work for them. I'll be paying each of you severance pay for three months to give you time to find other work."

Bruno steps up. "Who are the new owners?"

"The Leone family." Several of them gasp, recognizing the name.

"Drake did business with them?" Bruno's brow furrows.

"He wasn't aware of who they were at the time. Otherwise, he would've never signed an agreement with them." I run my hand down his arm, trying to ease his mind about Drake. "I'm so sorry that it's come to this. I tried my damndest to not lose this place if nothing else but for the sake of each of you."

Sofia chimes in. "I can attest to that." She locks her arm with mine. "Thank you for all the hard work you've put into this place. You're more like a family than an employee."

"Where will you go?" Gia asks Sofia.

"I'll be joining my sister in Essex for a new adventure."

"We're going to miss you so much," Gia sniffs and hugs her.

"I'm going to miss you too. You can always come for a visit, and if you ever want to leave New York, I'll have a place for you to work."

"We might just take you up on that offer." Bruno purses his lips.

"The three of you are always welcome." I pat Gia's slight baby bump.

Sofia and I tell each of them thank you and goodbye individually and watch them leave.

I glance at the time. "We really need to go, or we're going to miss our flight."

"Did you get everything packed?"

"Yep, it's loaded in Luca's trunk, and he's waiting for us out front."

She opens the front door, and I glance over my shoulder to the table where I first noticed Ever, and my heart sinks. "Goodbye," I whisper and walk outside and watch Sofia lock up one last time.

We both crawl in the back seat, and I see tears slip down Sofia's cheeks. "I'm sure going to miss this place."

"I know you will, but it will be good to have you back home." She lays her head on my shoulder, and we're quiet for the rest of the ride. Right before Luca pulls into the departure lane at the airport, his phone rings, and he puts it on mute.

"Yes, sir, I have it with me."

Part of me wants to snatch the phone from him and tell Ever that I love him; the other part says it will only make things harder for both of us.

"I will," he says, then hangs up.

He pulls up to the drop-off area, puts the car in

park and gets out, popping the trunk open taking out our luggage.

"Thank you for everything you've done for me." I hug his neck. "And, thank you for always being there for Ever. He needs you."

"He needs you more," he says, then pulls an envelope out of his pocket. "He asked me to give you this."

My hand shakes as I take it from him. I stuff it in my bag and hug him one more time. "Take care of him and yourself."

"You have my number if you should ever need anything."

I nod and help Sofia load our luggage on a cart. Then, I lock my arm with hers and walk through the double doors, but not without glancing over my shoulder and smiling at Luca. "Tell him I will always love him."

FOR THE PAST TWO YEARS, my world has consisted of one pertinent word: *After.* - Continue reading...

Never Ever After

THE NEXT BOOK IN THE SERIES.

NEVER EVER After

BESTSELLING AUTHOR
KELLY MOORE

PLAYLIST

Never Say Never by Cole Swindell, Lainey Wilson
    She by Jelly Roll
    Red Flags by Josh Ross
    Wreckage by Nate Wilson
    Son of a Sinner by Jelly Roll
    If You Want Love by Jon Langston
    Silhouette by Caleb Hearn
    Trouble by Josh Ross

ABOUT THE AUTHOR

"This author has the magical ability to take an already strong and interesting plot and add so many unexpected twists and turns that it turns her books into a complete addiction for the reader." Dandelion Inspired Blog

www.kellymooreauthor.com to join newsletter and get a free book.

Armed with books in the crook of my elbow, I can go anywhere. That's my philosophy! Better yet, I'll write the books that will take me on an adventure.

My heroes are a bit broken but will make you swoon. My heroines are their own kick-ass characters armed with humor and a plethora of sarcasm.

If I'm not tucked away in my writing den, with coffee firmly gripped in hand, you can find me with a book propped on my pillow, a pit bull lying across my legs, a Lab on the floor next to me, and two kittens running amuck.

My current adventure has me living in Idaho with my own gray-bearded hero, who's put up with my shenanigans for over thirty years, and he doesn't mind all my book boyfriends.

If you love romance, suspense, military men, lots of action and adventure infused with emotion, tear-worthy moments, and laugh-out-loud humor, dive into my books and let the world fall away at your feet.

ALSO BY KELLY MOORE

Never Ever Duet

Whiskey River West

Whiskey River Road

Elite Six Series

The Revenge You Seek

The Vigilante Hitman

August Series

Epic Love Stories

For more follow me on Amazon for a detailed list of books.

Printed in Great Britain
by Amazon